Forever Fifteen

by Cody Pierce

1 -

The moon shone over a deep black river, gleaming mockingly, yet beautifully over a bridge. Skies told him that it was almost dead midnight, dead night-time, dead dusk and the rain told him that the Gods were disappointed, disapproving of him. The bridge itself was ugly, broken, and covered in graffiti from the chipped concrete floor to the other side of the wall where the danger led.

He always wondered how they got the graffiti on the other side of the bridge without falling off. Did they use ropes? People? Did they jump off one at a time, armed with a hundred men to paint one line of artwork each, then die a sudden and forgettable death? He thought that sounded a lot more poetic than the first two. Imagine hundreds of people dying for one word, one name.

He sighed and stumbled pathetically to the edge. He tried hard to appreciate the pretty views; white angelic light burning bright against a contrasting black slime of dirty water but.. it was like he just didn't have it in him anymore. It was unfair that midnight was the only time his world looked so beautiful, but maybe it was because he couldn't see it. Midnight. His parents would kill him if they knew he was out this late. His parents would kill him if they found out he had gone back to his old habits. His parents would kill him. Metaphorical.

The gleams of the moon made him feel something. Something the boy hadn't felt for a while - he didn't know what it was, but what he did know is that he wanted more. He slowly, cautiously, calmly, climbed onto the stained wall that separated him from certain death. He sat impatiently on the wall, expecting the unexpected and wishing for some miracle. He wished, wished to travel someplace else - like a star, or the moon. Somewhere his thoughts couldn't follow him. He stared into the sky and silently begged the universe to take him to any place other than this. He had been here too many times before - too many nights, spent exactly like this. Night after night after night after night. But only this one was different. This time, this time, it was the end. He had done *too much.*

Atlas breathed out slowly, and lit a cigarette. What a way to spend his last few moments, choking on an addiction that wasn't even quick enough to kill him. It didn't even make him feel warm and fuzzy anymore, it just stopped him from being ill. He used to feel a spark like the lighter he lit the cigarette with, but that spark had long gone. He smoked until he couldn't feel his feet anymore, finally burying the cigarette but into his leg when he had coughed out the last breath. He knew it was time. Time to stop everything he hated. Everything he had ever loved.

The boy stood. His entire body was calm, collected, and ready. He was *ready*. He got up without a shiver, more confident than he had ever been in life, and threw down a notepad and pencil onto the dusty gravel. Atlas put a small sunflower there, letting it land safely next to the other items, next focusing on the black slime-like water. If he could have one wish, he knew it would have been to share this moment to everyone he had ever known. Atlas wanted them to see and to recognise what was going on - maybe then they would care. It was impossible, he knew that. Maybe that was him attention-seeking. Where do people even draw the line? Attention seeking, or crying out for help? He shuffled closer to the edge.

Heaven or Hell? That was the question. What even is Heaven? What is Hell? Atlas smiled, knowing so well that no matter what, he would end up in 'the bad place'. Whatever the fuck that was. Maybe Hell was the act of reliving a life again, and again, and again for eternity. Maybe Heaven was just looking down at the mortals for eternity. Either way, it felt like both would be torture. Heaven or Hell. Hell or Hell. Or neither - Atlas grimaced. The Boltzmann brain theory - after life, our consciousness ends up in deep space, formed by something and we watch the waves of nothingness. Forever. Atlas shook his head. There was only one way to find out.

His left foot stepped off the edge. Atlas braced himself, and got ready to jump.

Three.

The fall would take a while - perhaps thirty seconds of falling? Would it feel like less, or more? When he jumped - would that be when he regrets it all, and wishes he never did it? Bullshit.

Two.

He anticipated the icy cold water. It would puncture him, like tiny thousands of knives and pins pricking into his body. Maybe the cold itself would take him out, at once. If not, then.. the impact would kill him. Water is just as hard as concrete, from where he was falling from. It would smack him, sending shockwaves through his entire body.

One.

"WAIT!" a voice cried out from the shadows. Atlas felt his entire body start panicking. Blood rushed to his heart. It made him feel sick. He started shaking everywhere uncontrollably as thoughts pierced him. *What if this voice knew him? What if it was a police officer? What if they would tell someone?!* He felt tears piercing down his cheek, the salt prickling angrily into his injuries that corroded his face. Atlas turned away from the voice, intending to finish what he started. The shadow couldn't hurt him if he did it first.

"You're really going to do this."

The simple words made him freeze. *Was he going to do this?* Atlas knelt, knowing fully well one gust of wind would knock him off balance and off the bridge. Was he going to do this? He didn't do it the other nights.. what made him change his mind now? *No, he knew what he did. He was evil. He was a monster.* Atlas looked around for the voice, his eyes running side to side, panicked for an answer. *Who was this? Why did they care about him?*

A foot stepped slowly out from the shadows like a ghost, slowly, slowly walking towards Atlas. There appeared an old man, about seventy or so with lightning shaped wrinkles etched into his face. The wrinkles showed his warm smile, a ghost of a golden laugh - but his frown was powerful and stern. Atlas recognised his own advantages against the man's - in case he had to make a get away without terrifying the old man. The man was small, tiny, and had a bent back with a walking stick. He could barely look up at Atlas who was standing so scared on the wall. The man stepped closer.

"Don't come any closer! I- I don't want you to see this!" Atlas tried sounding confident, able, and commanding; but his tone told a different story - of a boy so terrified and dead, of a boy needing to be comforted so badly, or of a boy so desperate for a feeling he'd spend almost every night drawing blood from his thighs, a feeling he couldn't resist. He locked eyes with the old man, and for a split second Atlas saw the man's eyes widen at the state of Atlas's face.

The old man stepped closer again, and spoke clearly again. "My granddaughter was just like you."

He smiled softly at Atlas and carried on.

"Yes- she was just like you. A small child torn apart by the world. She thought there was nobody there for her. You're just the same, right?"

Atlas turned around to face the moon and tried blocking out the old man. He promised he would be gone today. He promised this would be the last time. If the cigarettes and ... other habits didn't kill him fast enough this was the only way. Atlas promised he would fucking end it. Tonight. Right here. Right now. Right. Now. It had to end. For everyone's sake because he was just a burden. A problem child. Nobody even loved him.. *so what was the point of trying?*

"She's my favourite grandchild. Of course, I can never say that to the others. But I think they all know it." He paused. "But alas, they're all old now. I think I've retired as a granddad. There's only an amount of ear pulling and entertaining I can do for a lifetime, and I reckon I'm out of it."

The boy swiped at his tears. "What's her name?" Atlas whispered, after hesitation.

"Her name is Annabel Lee. She means the world to me. Everyday when she was young, around nine, I would take her out of the house because her Mother, my daughter, would be stressed out of her goddamn mind, and we would go somewhere. It never really mattered where we went. We always had a great time. But... of course, we don't do that anymore."

Atlas looked around at the old man. He realised with sudden embarrassment that the old man was crying. Not loud sobbing, gentle, silent tears. It hit him like a punch to the stomach to see the old man's tears trickle down his cheek. Atlas didn't know the man at all. Maybe that's why it shocked him so much. Atlas tried asking another happier question to stop the piercing awkward silence.

"Why don't you do that anymore? Maybe if you reached out she'd be happy to do it." Atlas smiled apathetically. But the old man only sighed.

"Well, I just don't think she could anymore."

"Is she like a teenager? How old is she? I know teenagers, we're just dickheads. We don't mean to be rude. Just.. you know. Tired. And sad." Atlas pressed on.

"She would be turning twenty-six tomorrow."

"Would be?"

A new tear of the old man's fell down onto the broken concrete. He smiled pathetically, and Atlas tried not to look at the man's trembling lip.

"She committed suicide on her sixteenth birthday."

Atlas turned back around quickly. He didn't want to see the old man's miserable face. The wrinkles that once resembled a never ending smile transformed into a war-torn face shaped by his ever lasting grief that he couldn't get away from. Did it follow him like an ugly thunderstorm? Or did he go chasing storms, because the feeling of going without would be so strange, so painful, so unfamiliar?

The old man's words stung him. It made him feel something new. But this wasn't good. This hurt. This lingered. It felt like a shot to the head when Atlas realised he was doing the same thing as Annabel Lee. What if his Father turned out to be exactly the same as the old man, all because of him? The guilt he would feel. The afterlife would never let it not haunt him. It would be a sin so unforgettable even the Devil would curse him for it. The boy had a deep hatred for his Father, but.. he couldn't wish this on him. It hurt.

Atlas collapsed onto the concrete wall. He thought for a second that he heard the old man take a huge breath of relief.

"Turn around," the old man requested sympathetically. When the boy moved to face him, the old man was right in front of him. With his arms stretched out.

At once, Atlas climbed off the wall and ran into the old man's arms. He buried his face far into the man's bony shoulders and sobbed. The old man was like a beacon of sunshine. He held on like a baby crying for its Mother. Holding onto this real thing, this real person. He planned to end it all tonight. But instead of feeling dead, he felt so, so fucking sad. So fucking *sad*. His heart was pounding against his chest, his adrenaline was striking across his entire bloodstream. Atlas couldn't help crying out apologies and sobs of his own self hatred that he just couldn't run away from.

"I'm so s- sorry. I'm s- so fu- fucking s- sorry." He cried. "I h-hate myself. I hate m- myself so fu- fucking much. I just wanted it to e- end. I d- don't want to hurt you. Or D- Dad. I don't w- want him to c- cry."

He repeated his cries of wanting to kill himself, over and over again, until his throat grew hoarse, hugging the old man tighter than Annabel Lee could had ever. Atlas felt so warm in the man's arms. He felt so warm in his arms. Even though his eyes were closed, he felt his world capturing new colours. Golds, reds, yellows, greens, blues. He felt. He felt it all. The world wasn't so black and white anymore. It was blue. Very blue. But it was a start. It was a start.

"I'm so fucking sorry. I'm so sorry about your Annabel Lee. I'm f-fucking sorry m- man." Atlas wept.

The old man said nothing, but he hugged the tall boy harder. He stroked his back like a Mother would her child and said nothing. The old man tried so hard not to imagine the tall boy as his Annabel Lee. His grandchild. His baby.

Atlas cried into his arms until he passed out at sunrise.

2 -

When he awoke, Atlas was confused. Last night was supposed to be the end. *Why was he still here? Why was he still here, alive, worried, and so disorientated? Where was he?*

It was when he saw the old man with wrinkles, sitting right beside him, that he realised what had happened yesterday. He had failed. *Failed* to end it all. He remembered all of last night, though it was like a dream. A *nightmare*. He was so close to jumping when the old man... ruined it? Saved him? Atlas didn't even know what to think anymore. If he really really wanted to die that badly, why couldn't he just do it right now? It was right there.

Atlas tried getting up, but his legs just refused - so tired both emotionally and physically. He wished he could drop dead, right then, right there, without any effort. He wished he never existed - then his family wouldn't have to suffer through the grief. Like the old man and his Annabel Lee.

He looked over to the old man, who, an hour ago, was trying so hard not to fall asleep - but now, he was out cold. Atlas took a moment to really appreciate the man. After all - despite making the boy fail his plans, the old man made him feel something. He made him cry. Atlas hadn't cried in... years? After a while of emotional wrecks, he just stopped feeling. The old man made him feel the world. Sure, it was blue. But blue is better than black and white, right?

Atlas sighed, knowing that this man saved his life, yet the boy didn't even know his name. He was just a random guy.

 The man was wearing a messy red collared shirt with checkers, the buttons barely stretching over his stomach. He tucked it into his dark brown trousers that were held up by a thick leather belt. He looked so normal. He looked like such an average old man. Atlas could have looked at him on the street and not even care. He was so normal; except he wasn't. Atlas realised, if you looked close enough, you could see his backstory in his eyes. His wrinkles. The way he walked. The way he communicated through his gestures, his mannerisms.

Atlas looked away swiftly when the old man made a twitch in his sleep. What would happen now? Would the old man take him to the police station to be handcuffed and taken to a psychiatric ward? Atlas had already been to one before - a while back, now. It was okay for the people around him. It really helped them. But the emptiness in the bright white rooms scared Atlas. The people in the bright white uniform freaked him out. Everyone there had the best intentions - to help him. But he just couldn't accept it. It was like being in a hospital for a problem you were just born with; there was no point being there, because nothing could've been done about it. Or maybe his problem was fixable, but the feeling of his issues not being there was so drastically unsettling he couldn't bear to accept any help.

He didn't like change. He hated it. When he was younger, maybe around eight, his older sister started coming out of the hospital more frequently. He hated the change of it, because it was never certain if she could go, if she could stay. And whenever she was home, his Mother would be stressing about her going back. And whenever she was at the hospital, his Mother would be stressing about what the family would do all together when she was home. Change wasn't ever good for him. *Ever.* He wished so deeply to go back to when he was four years old, but with the memories he has now. He could change so many things. Do so many things. *Fix everything.*

Atlas glanced sleepily over to the old man. His eyes were opening slowly. The boy knew that this was his last chance to make a break for it. To make sure he wasn't taken anywhere he didn't want to go. But he just couldn't bear to leave the old man alone, at seven in the morning when he just saved his life. He had to thank him. Or yell at him. Atlas hadn't decided yet.

"Good morning." The old man croaked from the opposite side of the wall. Atlas smiled awkwardly without looking at the man. He didn't want to look at him. He wished they could just both forget what happened last night. It would make everything a lot easier. "My name is Ernie, by the way. What's yours?"

Atlas stared at the elder, who was now holding out a hand for him to shake. He really did look like an 'Ernie'. If the boy imagined a man named Ernie, this would be the outcome - a soft, fat old man. What was an 'Atlas' meant to look like? 'Atlas' would probably look like a skinny, anxious teenager; and he fit that description pretty well.

"Oh. I'm Archie." Atlas lied through his teeth, reaching out to shake Ernie's hand. It was his number one fake name to give to strangers. When he used to go on chat rooms to talk to the old lady on Childline, Atlas just felt like he had to make a fake name. Maybe it gave him a bit of security. A sense of control. Even though the chat moderators were probably checking his IP the second he logged in. They knew his real name. But they didn't use it. This was his pathetic idea of *control.*

"Well, Archie, what are you going to do now?" Ernie questioned.

Atlas groaned out loud. *What was he really meant to do?* He left everything he had ever loved like it was the last time he would ever see it. His phone was smashed to tiny particles and was now floating somewhere in a drain, all his cigs and bottles were scattered around his room; because who needs a hiding place when there's nobody there to suffer a consequence? He had left one personalised note to someone. If anybody else found it... he'd be called an attention seeker, a freak, or even worse - he'd be taken seriously.

He didn't want to go home. But really, where else was there?

"Is home not an option for you, Archie?" The old man asked softly.

"It's not my first choice. But I might have to," muttered Atlas. Ernie exhaled sadly at this, and stood up.

"I wish I could help you further. My house is currently in shambles. But I'm sure, no matter what your parents have done or are going to do, they love you so much and want you back home. Take it from a Father and a Grandfather." Ernie smiled, offering a hand to help the boy up - even though Atlas was almost double his size.

"You've done enough," Atlas mumbled, almost daring to scowl at the old man. Maybe he was ungrateful. But the old man didn't understand how hopeless Atlas was feeling. It was like a pit in his stomach that was dragging him down to the floor - to lay there forever whilst all his family and 'friends' moved on with their lives. And he would stay there. Stuck. Wishing it was another time, another year. Wishing that time didn't go so fucking fast.

He took the old man's arm, almost dragging Ernie down with him. He stared at the old man with such annoyance at his own confusion. What was he meant to feel..? He didn't want to hurt Ernie's feelings.. after all, he was just a burdened old man.

"Thank you.. I think." He whispered.

Atlas grabbed the notepad and chucked it off the bridge, as far as he could, into the scummy water where nobody could ever find it. Maybe it was time to go home.

Ernie watched Atlas walk away cautiously, until he was properly out of his eyesight. Maybe it was time for Atlas to go home.

He left home about a week ago, when everything got a bit much. It started with the school ringing home about their son's behaviour there. Absences, detentions, suspensions, and failure to attend every single one of his punishments. Good grades were just out of the question, of course. It was true that Atlas skipped school a lot. He didn't really get bullied - that was last year - it was more the routine that killed him; wake up, walk to school, debate his existence while walking over the bridges, listen to some old moron for four hours straight in a small, cramped room with twenty nine loud dickheads, sit alone at break time, and rinse and repeat. It just went on, and on, and on, and on, without a singular fucking change. So about two months ago, he skipped a lesson. Then another. And another. Then he started skipping the afternoons. And again. After that, he attended morning tutor to get registration, then walked out of reception. And he repeated it. Finally, he stopped showing up to school what-so-ever. And he made a habit of it.

Nobody missed him. In fact, he didn't even think his classmates knew he existed. A year ago he was a fun person to mock for a bit of a reaction; but when you destroy a person so much it becomes less fun. They don't react anymore. They just accept it. Since then, people left him alone. In a bad way. Sometimes, Atlas would wish that somebody would just beat the shit out of him, instead of just ignoring him day after *fucking day* like he wasn't even *there*. He wanted to have just a bit of attention, even if it meant being hurt. From somebody. *From anybody.*

Therefore, for every school day he missed, Atlas would be found talking to anybody he could find. A stranger passing by, a teen on the internet, an old lady asking for directions, a man online that always loved talking to him. He gained friends, joined groups, started habits that he wouldn't have started in any other situation, and had just a tiny bit of fun. Yet, he had never felt lonelier in his life.

So when his parents received his alarming school report, they went mental. His bed frame was taken away from him and sold, as were all his childhood toys that he didn't even play with anymore - but it still felt like a part of him was being ripped out when he saw his favourite memories being sold onto another child. The only things left in his room were a desk, a pen, and a notepad. His phone that his parents got him was taken away, obviously. He didn't expect to see that until he was a grade A student in everything - but that wasn't going to happen. Atlas had many cheap burner phones that he used for... stuff, but he also had his own decent phone with all his contacts if he needed it. But that phone was now smashed up into a drain by the park.

His parent's reaction just broke him up even more. All his keys to outside the house were taken away from him to avoid any other sneaking out and he had no privacy. But this wasn't even the worst thing.

In his depression, Atlas found comfort in a staff member at school. Atlas didn't know what made him feel so comforted with his 'friend', but he felt so weirdly safe that he could tell him anything. He had to attend school - especially now that his Father was driving him to make sure he actually got in the school grounds rather than accidentally finding himself fourteen train stops away from the building. He attended school, but not any lessons. The teachers couldn't legally touch him... so they couldn't force him into lessons. He stayed with the teacher all day everyday - his name was Richard, and Atlas started to tell him everything. Of how shit he felt all the time, of how nobody knew he even existed, of how his sister's death was really starting to fucking get to him. One day, he overshared.

A lot of phone calls, meetings with staff, police interactions, and psychiatric 'help' later - and when he got home from it all Atlas decided to pack up and leave. His house never really felt like a home before, but now it felt like a prison cell. All his keys were taken away. All his security. There really wasn't much to take with him; a few of his old oversized clothes, a pair of woolly socks, and his Father's wallet all stuffed into an unused school bag.

But here he was, standing in front of number fifty-four Wallow's Lane with a sick trembling feeling everywhere in him. Atlas knew this was an awful idea - but he wasn't going to stay. Atlas left a note and he needed to take it back as quickly as possible.

3 -

Standing outside his childhood home, he had never felt smaller. It seemed like the building was towering over him, looming with such power Atlas couldn't help but just start to shake everywhere. He swore to himself he would never step foot in this place again.

Atlas climbed in through his bedroom window, on the second floor. It took minimal effort - seeing how the vines on the wall were overgrown and unkept and led straight to where he wanted to go. On his way up, a few cars beeped at him, either warning him to get down or telling the homeowner somebody was breaking in.

He entered the open window with ease, making sure to tread lightly on the creaking floorboards. Atlas saw that his room hadn't changed at all in the entire week he had been missing; empty bottles lay untouched where he left them, the razor was still poking out pathetically from underneath the mattress, and worst of all, every single one of his clothes were exactly where he put them. Atlas' Mother, in particular, would always move his clothes to one side of the room for him to put away someday. He never did - it infuriated her. His clothes were exactly where he put them. She hadn't picked them up.

Why, though? Did she want to leave the room how she saw it? Did she want to preserve it like a memory of her younger child, who was happy and not lost on a bridge? Like she wanted to remember the child she never really wanted. She didn't want to perfect and tidy the room. To tidy it would be to take away her memories of her child. Her lost child. The child that she didn't want.

Atlas knew he was thinking far too much into everything. He thought too much. Atlas wished every day that his brain would just shut the fuck up, for once, maybe only for a minute. His brain was like a hundred different tabs all on at once, every single one of them expresses a different thought, a dream, a song, a memory. There was far too much going on all the time - he just couldn't relax. It was hard to not overthink, especially when the people around him really did think so shit of him.

The boy picked up the razor and placed it in his back pocket. Maybe it was finally time to quit. It was hard not to run his fingers slowly against the blade, just to reconcile what it was like. It had been too long since he had done it. Too long not being the average human too long. Too long being three days. In those three days Atlas got to a point where he just didn't have the energy to do it anymore. It didn't even have the same effect anymore. But now he had energy.. No. No, he came here for a different reason. And Atlas promised to himself to throw it out.

Atlas walked over to his mirror. A dirty and fucked up boy stared back at him. His most noticeable feature was the scars etched everywhere around his tanned white body, up his arm, down his legs, and carved prominently up his face, etching into his lips, and up his cheeks. *Disgusting*. Apart from the scars - which was most of him, the boy was extremely skinny and his bones showed at every joint. Atlas brushed back his overgrown straight blonde hair, the fringe starting to cover his eyes a little bit. His brown was starting to turn a bit copper, with the time he was spending outside - unwillingly. He had dirt smothered all over his clothes and in his hair, it really was disgusting but it didn't matter to him. Whatever.

Atlas took a deep breath, then opened the door, walking into the room just opposite his. This was where the note was, and he needed to take it back as soon as he found it. He left it underneath the covers of her bed, where nobody would have touched it. The boy felt the fabric of the blankets and felt memories washing over to him like a powerful wave.

It had been so, so fucking long since this room was in use. He missed the sound of the door creaking slowly, showing Atlas that his sister was finally home. He missed the sound of her laughter gently echoing into the creaking floorboards when she was facetiming her friends. He missed being so pissed off by her stupid blasting music that just seemed to go on and on. It had been so long since he had heard her voice.

For only a second, he felt his heart stop. The note wasn't there. *Where was it? Nobody was meant to have seen or moved it? Where was it?!* It was supposed to be right there, in a blue envelope addressed to 'Lenore'. He couldn't move - paralysed in fear he knew that somebody had seen it. Who saw it, though? His parents? His younger brother? A guest? Or maybe he just misplaced it? But that was impossible! Atlas swore to himself, starting to pace around Lenore's room. Could it have been swept off the bed? No. Not even the side of the wall. Was it under the mattress instead? No. What about under a pillow? No!

Atlas stopped pacing with a jump when he heard the familiar sound - her door creaking. Shit. His six year old brother, Elliot, with pupils bigger than the sun, stared up at his big brother with a trembling lip. The child looked more like Atlas' Father, blonde curly hair and huge brown eyes. Elliot looked up at him with such admiring eyes that Atlas felt sick to his stomach.

"Your face... what happened to your face?!" He whimpered sorrowfully.

It felt like an hour of scared silence had passed before Elliot began to cry, and jumped into Atlas' arms.

"Did you come back for me?" Elliot sobbed into his older brother's arms.

"No- Elliot. Please, listen-"

"Mum and Dad said you were dead!" he wailed louder, holding his brother as tight as his little arms could; like Atlas would disappear again if he didn't.

Elliot didn't understand death. He was only mimicking his parent's reaction. Lenore's absence meant nothing to him. At first he questioned it, sitting at the door waiting for her to come home when they used to go out and play at the park together. His Mother didn't even need to tell him why she was gone now, he kind of just... accepted it. After a while he stopped asking when Lenore would next be out of the hospital, he stopped waiting at the door, and he stopped thinking about her at all.

He was different with Atlas. Elliot knew something wasn't completely right about his older brother; through the way his parents treated him, and how sometimes Elliot would be playing a fun game with Dad, then his Mother would scream out something like 'he's fucking done it again', then Dad would go running up the stairs - leaving Elliot to play by himself. Atlas was his favourite out of the two siblings, even though Lenore paid a lot more attention to him than Atlas did. Maybe it was the fact that he was a boy like Elliot, but still felt a lot like Mum as well. He was comforting to Elliot when he'd scraped his knee or one of friend was being a bit of a dick.

Atlas didn't know what to say. Keeling down, he pushed Elliot off him a bit more aggressively than he meant to.

"Me too." he coughed out. "What happened whilst I was gone?"

Elliot sat down clumsily, wiping the tears from his cheeks on his sleeves. "I did a bad thing." He mumbled whilst looking down at the floor, disappointed with himself. "I made Mum really sad." Elliot sniffed.

"What do you mean? What did you do?" Atlas questioned softly.

"I went into this room and I was just playing. Then I saw a note on the bed."

Atlas' stomach dropped. He didn't want to hear what happened next. But Elliot carried on.

"I opened the envelope because I thought it looked pretty and then I tried reading it. Mum heard me reading a little bit and took the letter away. Then Dad picked me up and put me in my room for the rest of the day."

Fuck. His parents read the message to Lenore. His *brother* read a bit of the message too. Trying so hard not to have a crack in his voice, he questioned his brother on what happened next.

"Well, I went to sleep. Then I woke up and the neighbour, Elizabeth, was babysitting me. Mum and Dad didn't come back for two days, I think. Atlas, what happened while they were gone? Did they try and get you back?"

Atlas stood up and attempted not to black out from panic. His heart was beating so fast it scared him, his entire body was shaking head to toe. They read the note. They fucking read the note. What was he meant to do now? His parents wouldn't rest until they found him and put him in another mental hospital. He wouldn't be allowed out the house. It'll be like a year ago all over again, when he wasn't allowed a speck of privacy. Treated like an unpredictable virus. A *plague*.

The boy left his younger brother in Lenore's room. His world was spinning and he needed to get the fuck out of this house, as soon as possible. Atlas felt so sick and anxious. He just wanted Lenore's 'spirit' to read his goodbye, he was such a fucking idiot. Spirits aren't even fucking real.. *what was he thinking?!* Atlas stepped cautiously back into his own room, taking a few things with him whilst he got closer and closer to his escape - the window. Why did he even come back home? He wished he begged the old man to take him to his house. What even was his name again? Ernie. Ernie saved his life and he wished he could've stayed with him.

From a distance, Atlas could hear a heavy scuffle of footsteps racing up the stairs. Fuck. His Dad must know that he was here. The boy picked up a bottle and chucked it in his bag as fast as he could, then putting a pocket knife into his trousers, and ran to the window when he saw the door slam open.

"ATLAS!" he screamed. "Stay where you are, right now. I've called the police and if you step foot outside this house you are going straight to a hospital." To the left of him, Atlas' Mum entered the room with tears in her eyes.

"Please don't make us do this, Atlas. Haven't you done enough?" She said quietly, but Atlas could hear every word. Every unsynced breath, every gasp for breath.. Atlas turned to face her slowly and as his eyes met hers, he saw his Mum's face turn into shock and a face of pure fear, terror. "Atlas.. your face. Your face..!" she cried in dismay.

Atlas said nothing, but ducked his head down. He didn't want anybody to see him. He was frozen, stuck in the motion of getting ready to climb out the window. He still had a chance. He could run from the police. He could do it again, right? He had a change of clothes.. a razor to change his hair..? Atlas looked from his Dad to his Mum. His Dad was more angry than sad, which pissed Atlas off - whereas his Mum looked scared, anxious, like she didn't know how to react. Like she had never seen him before. Atlas' Mum took a step forward, trying to reach a dangerous hand to him.

"We want to help you. But you just can't accept it! We have tried everything, you have to understand that! And then you go fuck off and write some shit like this-" Her voice started to raise threateningly, holding up the blue envelope that made Atlas come back there in the first place. "-and now we don't know what to do! You're not even dead, you fucking prick! You didn't even die! So you just wrote this to hurt us, and so you could get away with stealing from us without us knowing!"

Even if he knew what to say, he couldn't. Fear grasped his words and suffocated him. It hurt to breathe. It hurt to think. His Mum took another step forward, and the boy could see her damaged and angry eyes blazing against his.

"You're such a dick!" She screamed. "Atlas, you're a fucking curse on this stupid family! You're a curse!"

He sat, frozen. Her words pierced into him and he could almost feel his heart slowly, slowly shattering, falling into his black lungs.

"And why would you even write to Lenore?!" She yelled, shaking the envelope furiously near Atlas' face. "Guess fucking what, Atlas? She's dead. She isn't coming back. She is gone and she can't read your stupid little notes. When are you going to fucking grow up and realise that, like everyone else has?!"

Atlas felt his eyes watering. Her words attacked him like a dozen knives aiming directly for his heart. He felt a singular, smaller tear fall down his cheek. As it did, he saw a similar one on his Dad's.

"Don't cry. Don't fucking cry. You want to be a man? Be a fucking man, then." She said to the boy through her teeth. Atlas' Mum tore up the letter, leaving scraps all over his already messy room. She walked out the room, followed by his Dad, who looked like he didn't know what to feel anymore. Atlas looked down at the one surviving sentence out of his note to Lenore.

The note read; 'and I have absolutely no idea - I am afraid.'

4 -

Immediately after his parents had left the room, Atlas had grabbed his bag and climbed out the window. They definitely wanted him to leave. If they didn't, his Dad would have at least bordered up the window, or reattached the lock back on his door. Not even his own family wanted him anymore.

Atlas looked up to the skies, black and clouded over. He thought he saw a star, but it was just an airplane. He rested on a park bench, trying so very hard to block out what just happened. His own Mum was right - he was a curse, a dick, an attention seeker for not following through. Why, for Gods' sake, why did he not just jump that night? He should have ignored Ernie, the stupid old man. He should have just done it in the morning after. *He should have jumped.*

The boy took off his backpack, searching for a bottle of anything to fill up the loneliness in his body. He found only a small glass with just a drop left, which he drank quickly. Atlas got up off his bench and walked to a nearby twenty-four hours open shop, the one near the school that always got stolen from. Atlas always felt bad for the shop owners, but honestly it was their fault for opening a sweet, vape, and liquor store right next to a school.

The shop owner, a middle aged man, greeted him with hesitation as he walked through the door. Atlas could already tell the man was showing caution to the person entering - he had been all too familiar with people just like Atlas, stepping into the shop at midnight looking for only trouble. Was he going to steal something? This was a question that Atlas too was asking himself. Was it really worth screwing over this man just to supply his own shitty habits? No, he had money, he could pay.

Atlas fixed his posture and walked confidentially up to the checkout, and with the manliest, deepest voice he could, Atlas mumbled; "Can I get a packet of cigs and a bottle of that Smirnoff?"

The man took the bottle and cigs off the shelves and placed it on the counter, refusing to give it to the boy just yet. "Take your hood down, mate." The shopkeeper stopped for a second to take a closer, better look at the boy. After he looked at his face, the man seemed to tense up. With an uneasy voice, he followed up with another question: "Can I have some ID please, son?"

"I lost it," Atlas said, refusing to break eye contact.

"Look mate, we both know you're not eighteen. Not even close. Now get out of my shop before I call the police." The man said, annoyed. Normally he could tell from a mile away if the people wanting to be served were genuine or not, but there was something so unafraid and dead about this 'kid' that seemed so .. mature?

"No genuinely, please, I reckon I have it somewhere." Atlas pointed to his backpack, starting to slide it off his shoulders. "Whilst I find it, can you also get me that, please." He pointed to some sort of wine bottle at the very end of the protected shelves. The man grumbled under his breath, walking over to the wine section. Whilst he was there, Atlas sprang into action. He slid the bottle and packet into his backpack, and put on the counter a ten pound note - definitely not enough, but it was the thought that counted. When the man shouted at him to come back, Atlas had already ran halfway up the road. It didn't feel good to steal from him. But he had to admit, the adrenaline was really started to kick in, like a powering bass drum at a concert. He could've just kept the money too, but then he would've felt even worse. Whatever. It's fine. Stealing happens.

Atlas had stolen before, many times. But he always made sure to take from big companies that wouldn't feel the damage, whereas when people took from small family owned businesses it was just plain wrong. That's why he felt so bad. It's fine. He'd repay it another day. When he could afford it.

The boy trudged from the market road to the park again, where he opened the bottle pathetically. Imagine if all his relatives and friends - no, classmates - could see him now. Alone on a park bench with nobody to care for him and cuts all up his face drinking a flavourless Smirnoff. What a great fucking life to be living. But it was better than being at home. It was better than being at a party with fake people who try so hard to not seem like they are just there for the alcohol - which, shocker, they are. He took drink after drink, and after a while, the burning sensation felt more like an old friend he had missed for a long time. Soon, the world felt a little more simple. A lot happier. And really.. spin-y. Like it was only half loading in as he was looking around.

He reached into his pocket for the packet of cigs, but instead he felt the sharp metal that he picked up earlier. Atlas held it out in front of him, slowly watching the glare of light move around as he twisted it underneath the moonlight. He tried focussing on the stains he had made, but the spots kept moving around and he couldn't pinpoint where they were - were they even real at all? But whatever. The red stains weren't important right now. It was time to get rid of it, once and for all. Atlas got up without falling over, and walked around the places he knew so well, until he found a place unfamiliar. Maybe it was the drink, but even after living here this entire fifteen years of his life, he had never seen this passage way before. He closed his eyes, spun around cautiously, and felt the razor escape from his fingers. Without looking around to see where it went, he left the passageway.

Daylight approached the park at six in the morning - Atlas woke up still drunk to a golden sunrise. Was this his reward for surviving the night? Because he barely did that. When his soberness started to return halfway through the night, Atlas realised he was freezing to death and if he didn't do something about it, he wouldn't be alive the next morning. The boy made himself drunk again, to feel a bit warmer whilst his entire body was on the verge off switching off his heart was beating so slow. If he didn't wake up the next morning, what did he fucking care? It saved him a job, a job that he was finding annoyingly difficult to complete.

Though it was only around six, people were starting to show up around the park. Early morning joggers, dog walkers, friends catching up with one another, and business men and women walking around like they owned the place. When every one of them passed Atlas, it was like they sneered before taking a proper good look at him, then their eyes widening, then quickly walking off again. Maybe he was just feeling extremely paranoid, but it felt like the entire world was watching and judging him. He felt their eyes travel where he walked, he heard their conversation break off for a beat, then carry on - but this time quieter, reserved, whispering, like they were talking behind his back; or about him.

It was Atlas' own fault. He did this to himself. He made himself look like this. And it didn't seem to be going away. Atlas would have never called himself attractive; because he wasn't. But he hated how he looked, every day of his life, falling asleep next to mirrors was a common occurrence because he was so obsessed about what he did or didn't look like. Atlas' parents took down every towel he put up to cover up the reflection on the mirror, so he was forced everyday to meet his own eyes. Atlas was so fucking ugly to himself. He had weird teeth, stupid jawline, flat, greasy hair and a shit body. He was built like a skeleton - like somebody forgot to add the skin and muscle onto him before he was born.

Atlas didn't even know what he looked like anymore. His mind had built up some sort of different lookalike to him where all his characteristics he hated were so much worse than before, imperfections bursting out of the reflection. He hated it. Atlas fucking hated himself. But one day his disliking just went too far. In his opinion, he fixed his face. Not many people shared the same thoughts, though.

He sat up slowly, feeling a pounding to his head instantly. The question now was: where next? Atlas knew he had nobody close enough to stay with - and any family member was out of the question. Was his parents going to bother marking him as missing to the police? Maybe he could travel to another country on a train. Maybe he'd go on a train and see how long it would take for them to kick him off for not having a ticket - the boy could make it to Brighton and start a new life. But that was a child's thought. It wasn't actually possible.

Or was it? There were no repercussions his drunken mind could think of.. so why not? Worst comes to worst... he gets kicked off at some manky place like Birmingham. Atlas could do it. It'd be fun. An adventure, even.

Atlas stood up with a big stumble that somehow didn't land him back on the bench he almost died on last night, and made his way through the town. He moved in an out of alleyways - he was still in his parents' hometown, after all, he didn't want a scene in front of everyone. Except nobody was around. The train station wasn't far from the park, maybe about a fifteen minute walk if you were fast?

The boy heard voices approaching him from behind. Fuck. This wasn't good. Alone in an alleyway when nobody else was nearby to hear him. Atlas couldn't help but flick the pocket knife from inside his trousers. Just in case. The voices got louder and louder, when suddenly he was almost dead sure he heard group of four boys, who sounded and smelt really high.

"I swear- I recognise that jacket. Hey, mate, turn around!" The tallest one yelled out. It wasn't a request, it was an order. Atlas turned to face the four boys, and to his dismay he recognised three of them.

They were all taller and looked a lot stronger than him, that was at once the first thing he recognised. If they wanted, they could easily rob him and only one of them could definitely overpower him. But they didn't have a knife, Atlas did. The tallest boy was in the year above Atlas, and called Theo. He had black, straight hair and looked pretty skinny, but the boy knew that he was still tough. The other two he recognised were at the back, one was ginger and the other was blonde. And they all looked threatening.

"Hey," Atlas said, trying not to show his uncertainty. The boy turned around to start walking off again when Theo called out to him again.

"You were that kid that went fucking mental in the IT office weren't you?" Theo sneered, making the group all laugh. Atlas began to walk off. It was too early for this. Too loud for his hangover. Too much effort to be made fun of.

Suddenly, Atlas felt his hood being yanked off and Theo grabbing his arm.

"Don't fucking walk away from me when I'm talking to you, mate." He squeezed tighter. Theo forced Atlas to look at him, and then his own eyes widened. "The fuck did you do to your-"

The rest of the boys stared and howled with laughter. The smell of weed was radiating through the air with every breath they had to take through gasps of sneers. Atlas felt sick.

"What do you have in your bag? Can I have a look?" Theo smiled, starting to unzip it.

"I dare you to take anything from there and you'll see what happens." Atlas growled.

The group made an annoying 'oooo' noise at the comment, and the ginger boy shouted 'give *it* what *it* deserves'. But Theo just took his hands off Atlas and the bag. They stood there for a moment, nobody moving when Theo quickly swung a fist right into Atlas' face.

Atlas instantly crumpled to the group. His hangover wasn't helping at all, the world was spinning in three directions at once and it felt like he could never get up again. His cheek throbbed uncontrollably, and he felt blood seeping into his mouth. The aching stunned him for a minute, letting the boys gather round to make fun of him. Atlas coughed up blood onto their shoes, and lay his head pathetically against the wall behind him. What now? Were they going to beat him unconscious?

"That," spat Theo, "was for the trouble you caused me a year or so back."

They jeered at him as tried to get up, Atlas clutching at his face, dripping blood and saliva onto the ground. He only managed to crouch for a bit before collapsing on the floor again, which earnt more laughs from the boys. Why now? Why couldn't this have happened later... another time.. not when he was still drunk. Theo spoke again, softer this time. "Are you meant to be a boy?"

Atlas spat blood. "Yes." He said, not as confident as he wanted it to sound, glaring up at him.

"I bet you it's a tranny." one of the other boys taunted.

"I'm not. I swear- I swear I'm not."

"Why don't we prove it, lads?" Theo grinned.

No. No, this can't be happening. At six in the fucking morning. He knew what was going to happen. He knew what they were going to do. The boy he didn't know came closer to him. *Fuck*. This can't be happening. This isn't how he wanted things to go. Atlas felt the boy restraining his legs, and touching his trousers. Shit. What could he do? Why are they doing this? This can't be happening. *Please. Make it stop.*

The boy shoved him tightly into the wall, he couldn't move an inch. *This can't be happening. Not here. Not now.* A shiver down his legs warned him, the boy was grabbing at his clothes, pulling them away.

Not like this, not like this. I have to do something. Don't touch me, leave me, leave me.

Atlas felt for the knife in his pocket, and without a hint of hesitation slashed against the boy's hand shallowly. The shock of the pain was enough to snatch his hand away, angrily gaping at the small scratch Atlas has caused. With a wave of dizziness, Atlas jumped up with all the power he had, and held the knife out in front of them.

"Get the fuck away from me. *Get the fuck away, don't come any closer!*" Atlas screamed at them. He backed away from the group, holding the knife out with both hands - so tightly because he knew his life depended on it. Whilst the others backed away, Theo took a step closer.

"You think you're all big and threatening just cause you have a knife? You need a fucking weapon to seem a little dangerous. You should sit back down and put that away before you hurt yourself. Again." Theo sneered, looking at the cuts on Atlas' face. He walked over to him and tried disarming him.

"Fuck *off*. Don't fucking *touch me!*" Atlas hissed through his teeth, moving his arms away from him. It was now or never. *Hurt him*. His body wasn't moving. *Do it*. He would've done so much worse to you. *Stab him*. It's so easy - he's right there. *Cut him. You know you want to. Do it.*

Atlas seized Theo's arm and stabbed with all his power into him. Blood spurted in all directions, showering the already stained concrete with thick, dark red blood. Atlas felt vomit creeping up his throat, but resisted quickly, pulling the knife out of his arm and holding it back out in front of him.

Theo shrieked at the sight of his arm and fell onto the ground, shuffling as fast as he could away from Atlas. He felt no pain - the adrenaline was keeping him alive, but the sight made him feel faint.

"What the fuck-! You piece of shit..! You're fucking mental-!" The boy screamed, trying to shuffle away on the floor without brushing his bloody hand anywhere. The other boys looked around at each other, uneasy, not knowing what to do, and helped him up in a hurry, running back out of the alley. Atlas had done it.

Atlas had done it. Avoided.. the boys. Avoided.. them.

He peered down to his hands, which were stained with Theo's blood and dirt, though he wasn't sure which one was which. He *stabbed* someone. Theo was right. He was *fucked up*. Who stabs other people? But it was self defence. He didn't have to stab him for it though. It was necessary.. he was going to do stuff.. Atlas didn't have to do it that deep, though. Right?

Flipping the pocket knife back down, Atlas vomited up what was left of the metallic vodka.

5 -

'This is the southern service to Brighton, calling at SouthBourne, Chichester, Durrington, Worthing, East Worthing, Hove, and Brighton.'

Despite all the exhausting events leading up to the train, it wasn't easy getting to sleep. Atlas was completely alone in the carriage, yet he felt eyes staring, glaring at him and getting ready to attack him.

The morning's incident was haunting him. The group of teens' words were pounding against his head, and he could still feel that boy's dirty fingers pressing down firmly on his thighs, he could still feel Theo's hands grasping tightly on his arm. But worst of all, he still felt the knife's metallic edges, the feeling of vomit creeping up his throat when the red exploded everywhere. He still felt the feeling of stabbing into Theo's wrist. *It was his own fault.*

Every jolt of the train made his entire body jump about a mile, every door opening made him look around rapidly. The people who passed him didn't even look at him; but Atlas still found a way to be anxious about them. He had done bad things before. He was a shit person. A curse.

"We are now approaching Worthing. Please mind the gap.'

So far, he had been able to stay on the train without a ticket. A worker had come into the carriage, but she had taken one sympathetic look at the hooded teenager, and left the carriage without interrogating him for his ticket. So far, she was the most helpful person to Atlas in a long, long time. Atlas didn't really care if they came to him, though. What else could they really do to him? Did they care about their job that much? Or was it just the power over other people that they liked? Either way, it was bullshit and Atlas decided it was beneath him. So Atlas would:

one, ignore the person, or two, just run off at the next stop.

What was he going to do in Brighton? What was there to do in Brighton? That is, of course, if he even made it. Twenty-five minutes to Brighton without being taken off by a worker. That seemed possible. He could find a shelter to stay in, or just camp it out in the park by the anti homeless benches, armed with a bottle of vodka, a pack of cigarettes, a bloodied pocket knife and forty quid to his name. What a luxury.

Maybe he could get a job. An easy job. Perhaps as a café worker in some sketchy independent place down the lanes. Five pounds an hour. Forty hours a week - more depending on how dodgy that place was. With that money he could bribe some flat owner to let him bunk down for a bit. After that, he'd make some friends, and maybe even meet a special person, who he'd get really close with and start a relationship with.

Then what? Then... then he would find a real place to stay. Then he'd probably end up killing himself several days later.

Fuck, it was so *futile*! So *pointless*! What was the point in getting all this money, working so hard when Atlas knew, not that deep down, that it wasn't worth it?! He was going to end up dead a lot sooner that most people planned for him to. Why should he work forty fucking hours a week when it was going down the drain, or rather, down into the funeral service. It was so useless trying.

Atlas banged his head against the train window. Why was he even coming to Brighton? He should be under the train, not in it. There was honestly no point for him in this world, and he fucking knew it. He didn't have the energy to end it all. He just wanted to sink into the train floor and stay there.

The doors opened, and Atlas whipped his head round. Fuck. A worker. They made direct eye contact, and he came walking straight over to wear Atlas sat.

"Ticket please, mate."

"Lost it." Atlas croaked.

"It's eight in the morning and I've already heard that five times and I'm not falling for it. Do you have one or not?" He waited for a moment, but Atlas just stared straight ahead, trying to ignore him. "I'll take that as a no. Are you under sixteen? If you are, you get a cheaper ticket. Or, if you have a student pass, it's a bit less too. But if you're not going to pay, I'll have to fine you fifty quid. What's your name, lad?"

"Archie."

'We are now approaching, East Worthing.'

The boy got up from his chair, and walked away from the man. He ignored the worker calling out, annoyed, and waited at the door. East Worthing was close enough. If he wanted to go to Brighton that bad, he could just take another train. Or walk there.

'Stop, boy!' He said sharply, coming towards Atlas. "I'm trying to help you!"

'This is my stop.' He spoke quietly, then pressed the button to get off the train. It wasn't the right thing to do, maybe, but he had limited money. Atlas couldn't waste it on tickets.

The worker could have ran out the carriage and called security to grab him, but he didn't. He stood silently at the door, watching the boy walk away, lost. The worker knew this wasn't his stop. He knew he had just made this boy get off somewhere unfamiliar, random to him. It was his job. It doesn't matter.

Atlas found himself lucky. The train station was barely a station at all, really just a strip of concrete with two waiting benches. It was an underfunded station with no gates. Luck was finally on his side, for once. Walking out of the 'station', he grimaced, annoyed at the anti-homeless benches that the county had made the money for. Really fucking saving lives out here.

The sun was fully up now, being enclosed in dirty grey clouds, but still blazing into Atlas' skin angrily. It was an unnaturally hot day in autumn. Atlas explored Worthing with extreme disliking. The limited supply of trees were turning golden and orange, familiar colours that reminded him of last year, falling, falling, then forgotten on the pavement. Autumn was always shit. There was never any exceptions. He couldn't remember a single good day.

The more he looked around, the more his stomach grumbled at him. When was the last time he had eaten? His lips suddenly felt very cracked and his throat infuriatingly dry. When was the last time he drank water, or just any liquid that didn't make him drunk? He had money. Limited. But he had money.

Around the town were candle shops, a church, and an off-licence news agency. He needed food. Atlas kept walking, though he felt himself slowing down scarily fast, dehydrated and starving. His only food consisted of cigarettes and blood. He was tired, and just about to give up when he saw a chip shop labelled 'Sunny Side Chips', right next to the seafront. It wasn't really what he was going for, but it would have to do.

Stepping in, he realised he was the only one there. It took a painful five minutes for somebody to turn up on the counter, lamely asking him what he wanted. He felt the judgement through every drawl of speech she mumbled. He had to supress a huge urge to smash his head right into the glass that separated the two.

Atlas sat down and waited. He always liked imagining what people's lives were like. He imagined that girl - the nametag said Sadie - to only work to get out of her house. Maybe she had to care for a younger sibling or something, but she couldn't be bothered and decided getting a job was easier than staying at home and making tired conversation with the inner family. He thought that she was the type of girl to be popular, and yet desperate to not be in the attention's eye.

What would someone say about his life? Most people would definitely say drug dealer - due to the constant hood being up, and the stench that followed Atlas everywhere from the boys' weed.

Atlas stared over into the grease stained mirror. How did this fucking happen? His hair was matting a bit, and there seemed to be dirt streaking all over his face and clothes. Blood was still stained to his jacket dripping onto the floor from his mouth. No wonder that girl, Sadie, looked him up and down in disgust.

Atlas would do the same. *I mean, just look at yourself.* Blonde hair that was turning black from the muck and grease building up, ripped up clothes and a fucked up face. What else was wrong with him? That stupid resting bitch face that deserved a punch. Skinny arms that were somehow still holding blood despite all he did to himself. Fat fucking thighs that were bumpy and scarred.

It was so hard to not be disgusted with himself. How could he even go outside looking like this? It was so hard to not strike the mirror down. Every other second he kept looking, it felt like another thing was morphing like a tumour and making up new parts of his face that he never remembered a minute ago. But he was there. And he was so disgusting. It was so hard to not vomit right there and then.

How can he live like this? It must be so embarrassing to everyone around him. To be seen with him. It had been three years. Three fucking years and he still needed to wait, threemore until he could change himself. Is three years waiting for? *What if everything went wrong and he still hated himself?* Then all that waiting was for nothing. *What if he can't even fix himself after they're done? If nothing changed?*

Atlas couldn't help it. He brushed and poked against his pale, monster like skin and wished he could be in somebody else's body. Years of waking up still alive after a wishful dream of dying peacefully in his sleep, he was still in his own deteriorating body. He'd take anybody's body. Maybe even Sadie's. Anybody's, please, just anyone's, except his own. He'd go to be a girl if it just meant that he could stop being... him.

The boy wanted to scream. For someone to take away the boy staring back at him in the reflection. He wished it wasn't him. That it was all a bad dream. That he could start again. Fix his face. Fix his life. Fix the past.

His body wasn't his own. His mind and body fought against each other, worse than any war he was ever taught about. His mind craved love and a difference. His body cried and wanted love. But the two jigsaws got mushed up together in alcohol and self hatred, a long time ago, so badly that they just didn't go together anymore. This body meant nothing to him. Nothing at all. Nothing. It meant nothing. Like everything else about Atlas' life.

"Hey!" Sadie calls out, clearly irritated. Atlas looked over in a hurry. "Gods' sake mate, I've been calling you for a minute now."

She stepped over to Atlas with his chips, and almost threw them down in front of him. Atlas wanted to smile at her, say thank you, any sort of gesture; because he felt like he just knew her. But the sound of his failing, croaking, awful voice stopped him.

The amount of times he'd try screaming his voice hoarse, only for it to come back a couple hours later. That was one of the reasons he never stopped smoking, too - it decreased his voice pitch. It drove him to insanity, the scratchy throat feeling, but it was worth it. Now he hadn't smoked in a while, he felt his hand jittering from underneath the table and his squeaking voice creeping back on him now.

When he couldn't smoke for a bit, Atlas went completely mute. The sound of his own voice made himself feel sick. The smoke was like some sort of barrier slotted into his lungs that saved him from the anxiety it caused him. Stupid. It's not real, anyway. Just dumb withdrawals.

Atlas felt his stomach rumble loudly. He peered over at his chips, and ate a few.

His mind flashbacked suddenly to a lonely Friday afternoon, when he had been sent home for vomiting into a class bin - suffering from a painful migraine. He was crouched uncomfortably, head facing into the toilet bowl, readying himself for another wave of sickness.

He remembered looking down, and not seeing a discomforting shape morphing in and out of his view. Instead, he saw his stomach. And it was so flat. So perfect. He loved his body just a bit too much from when he was completely empty.

Empty. Hungry, starving. And ill. Very ill.

Atlas ran out of the shop, food untouched, three pounds fifty wasted.

Waves crashed gently at his worn out feet, soaking them completely through holes and rips in the cheap materials. Atlas sat on a wooden pier, looking deeply into the scummy water which he couldn't see the bottom of. Water splashed against the pier repetitively, showing a smooth and detectable pattern; Atlas tried taking it all in. It was meant to be calming, but there was a nagging type feeling going on in his brain, trying to activate his fight or flight - but he couldn't find the energy nor adrenaline to recognise it.

His feet were aching uncontrollably - since he had been walking along the seafront for about two hours now, but the numbing cold of the sea was getting rid of the pain, just a little bit. There were people around, although they were far back on the shore, and none of them took any interest into Atlas - who was sat, alone, and hadn't moved since he got there, an hour ago.

He tried, with failure, to not see the similarities between the two times he was sitting near water recently. He tried, without success, to not think about the night he wanted to revisit over, and over, and over, to tell himself he was making a huge mistake by listening to that stupid old man. Why didn't his brain just shut up? If he should be dead, why couldn't his brain just take over and do it for him?

Pictures of his childhood flashed through his mind, reminding him of what he was missing back at home. Has Elliot stopped asking for Atlas yet? Has his Dad gotten over it? Has his Mum forgiven him? Has Lenore... has she... Fuck. He should have visited her grave before leaving. When was the last time he went there, of his own free will? He didn't want to think of the answer. It sickened him.

He threw a rock into the sea - seeing it ripple out slowly, he threw another. And another. And another. Anything to distract him from the fact he had only bothered seeing his sister three, maybe four fucking times before having to leave her forever. How long would it be until he was back where the graveyard? Would he ever see her again? What was he thinking, what did he say the last time he saw her - did he know it would be months before he was even thinking about seeing her again? But that wasn't fair. The dying flowers and cracked stone signs weren't her. They weren't Lenore. Lenore was a shining sunflower in the sunlight, laughing and crying and making sounds of joy, sounds of life. Lenore was the refreshing, cool breeze in a hot summer's day. Lenore was an angel, full of love to give. She was the most innocent person, but Death stole her away - greeting her, adding her to His company.

Death didn't take her, though. Encephalitis did. When she was diagnosed with it, Atlas couldn't even pronounce the word. Now, it stuck to his throat like a tumour and grasped against his lungs by just the thought of it. Elliot could barely talk when she was diagnosed. Lenore was sick for weeks - it started out as symptoms of the flu, but it got gradually worse and worse, and by the time the doctors caught on, it was too late. All they did was trap her in a hospital for weeks on end and try out new medication. And then, she had her first seizure. It was her last.

What a way to die. Shaking, jolting, having no control of her body, and choking on her own sick. She died right there, in her bed, at home, all alone. They said there was nothing that anyone could have done. That it was better than her suffering. Better than her dying in the hospital. Better than her going insane from eventually not being able to talk, to function, to love like Lenore was so used to doing. But Atlas knew better. When it happened, Atlas was in his room, giving into his habits and not caring for his sister. He could have saved her. Called his parents before she vomited. Got her facing any direction except upwards. But no. He was in his room, hurting himself because he never wanted to hurt anyone else;

but by doing so, Atlas practically murdered his Lenore. His angel. His cool breeze. His shining sunflower.

It was all his fault.

Atlas couldn't hold his anger at himself anymore. He scratched his nails into the wood and screamed. Screamed with all his self hatred, flowing out into the waves that were meant to be soothing. He screamed until his voice went hoarse. Screamed until his nails tore off his fingers, drawing blood fast. His pain didn't matter. He'd take all the pain in the world forever to bring back his Lenore. He'd take all her pain, all her illness. Just for one more laugh. One more smile. One more memory of childhood.

He couldn't stop his tears falling, pricking against all his wounds. It was like a reminder that he deserved the pain. How was it possible to feel so much disgust against himself?

The boy yelled himself hoarse until he felt his fingertips releasing against the splintering wood through fatigue. Did anyone even care? Did they want to help him? He looked around. Everyone was gone.

He climbed down from the pier, back onto the shore and through the streets. His feet formed sore blisters over older ones, it took most of his energy not to start limping in the side of the road. That would be pathetic. Atlas walked and walked, looking for anything that could actually help him; a homeless shelter, a fire department, maybe even a soup kitchen. People took pity on suffering children, Atlas had to take advantage of that - even if he knew he didn't deserve it.

Walking. Walking. Walking. His entire body ached; his bones creaked like they were screeching at him to please, stop, to let himself rest. He didn't give in until he collapsed onto the floor in a sudden heap, whilst the people all around him wandered on, trying not to look at the boy too much.

Cold. It was cold. Atlas knew it was freezing. He could almost taste his own icy breath stretching against his lips. But he was dreaming. Dreaming of a familiar chill, one that included Christmas, pretty lights, and warm cocoa. The numbing frost he felt right now was real, but harsh and interrupting. Atlas felt gentle drips of rain pouring down on him, slowly at first but then getting faster and more powerful which only made him more cold. He couldn't break out of his dream. He didn't want to. It was too tiring. He just wanted to stay there, to the side of the pavement forever and die quietly, to the side of the pavement, where nobody would care to check on him.

All of a sudden, the rain stopped; but he still heard it thundering down all around him. He also felt a strange warmth to the front of him. A muffled voice got more noisy the longer he tried to ignore it; he was slipping back into consciousness.

"Hello? Are you okay? Are you alive?" a voice repeated over and over, until it saw a flicker of Atlas' eyelid.

Atlas opened his brown eyes cautiously. He was exactly where he was when he passed out, to the side of the pavement - next to the road and the fences that guarded the beach. Clouds were now grey and clouded over, forcing the sun away which made Worthing seem a lot more mucky and depressing than it really was. The people stepping quickly were still ignoring his existence, except now there was somebody right in front of him.

The boy felt an anxious chill run down his spine. He reached for his knife in a hurry, but kept his hand there when he saw that the person wasn't a threat at all - she was a young woman holding a rainbow umbrella above both their heads. Her hair was navy - black, curly strands running all down her back and she looked beautiful. She seemed perfect - her nose was button-like, her lips full and uncracked, and she looked clean; something Atlas wanted to be badly. The girl's skin was lovely, deep browns and splodges of white around her golden left eye and down by her right cheekbone, stretching all the way to her neck. She looked unnatural, peculiar, but graceful and pleasing at the same time.

"Thank Gods for that. I thought you were dead." She cried out through a happy grin. Atlas noticed she had a smiley piercing that made her even prettier when she beamed. "Here, let me help you up." The girl reached out her hand to pull him up, but Atlas retreated at the sight of it; clutching dearly to his knife. She quickly recognised his discomfort, and crouched down to his level - sitting on the wet gravel with him.

She coughed awkwardly, but kept talking. "I'm sorry. I'm very outgoing, I guess! People say that about me a lot. Do you talk?" Atlas merely nodded, and she laughed. Not mockingly. In a soft way. "Well you're not doing a great job of it. Can we start properly? My name is Eulalie. My friends call me Lee. What's your name?" Eulalie spoke so quickly, like she was in a rush - or maybe that she had so much to say in her brain but the girl just couldn't get it all out in time.

Eulalie reached her hand out again, and this time, something that was in that girl made Atlas accept it. She pulled him up with ease, staring at his figure up and down, up and down. When her eyes met Atlas' face, she didn't jump back in horror, or wince in disgust like others did. Instead, Atlas noticed a cloud of pity and sadness circling her golden eyes. He looked down to the ground in embarrassment.

She paused for a moment, before turning a lot more gentle than before. "Hey, it's okay. Me too." Eulalie spoke softly, "I'm getting better, though. I mean, kind of. I hope you are too. If you want to get better, that is."

Atlas smiled, even though it hurt him to do so. This girl.. she could help him. She might have somewhere to stay. Somewhere to eat. To be safe. No, that was far too hopeful. She'll probably be leaving-

"So, do you need somewhere to sleep? As comfy as it looks, I don't really think I'd be able to live with myself if I let you stay out here." Eulalie smiled.

Atlas nodded, staring at the concrete floor he had passed out on. "I need to know your name at least. You know mine, so I guess it's only fair."

"Archie." he lied. There was something so personal with his name. He didn't want anybody new speaking to him with it. It reminded him of the last couple of months. It was time to leave them behind, and it started with that stupid name. Even though Atlas knew that he'd never be able to forget. The dates, months, memories were built into him, programmed to make him miserable.

She began to walk to the busier side of the city, Atlas stumbled and struggled to keep up with her power walk. What was he meant to say to her? Was he even meant to talk? It seemed like she liked talking. But was he allowed to do it back? Was it more of a talk out loud, no response kind of thing? Or did he have to input his own statements, opinions?

"Why don't you talk much?" she asked, stopping to stare back at the boy who she had just realised was limping behind her.

"It hurts to."

"Why did you do it?" Eulalie cocked her head, a bit like a confused dog or something. Atlas shrugged.

"Oh come on!" she pushed on. "I used to always have a reason. Like, if I had a bad day, or, like, if my friends were being bitchy, or if I was pissed. But we're so over that now, yeah? And that." she said, pointing to the carved wounds on Atlas' face. "You have to have a reason for *that*!" she exclaimed, sadness lingering in her voice. Atlas couldn't help but turn red from the self-consciousness he felt burning into his cheeks. People were looking. Eulalie was loud.

She saw Atlas' head sink a bit, quickly rushing to say: "Oh my gosh, I am so sorry. I'm a bit personal sometimes! I really don't mean to be, I promise not to do that again!" she spluttered out, her face blushing and hands covering her mouth in surprise of herself - even though she most likely apologised for this twice a day.

"Come on, my flat is this way." she said.

7 -

Atlas took the spare 'bedroom', which was a pull-out sofa in the living room. The sofa was scratchy, had stains everywhere, and was half broken; but it was somewhere to sleep. The first night he woke up to Eulalie shouting a song at about five in the morning, dancing around her kitchen, tapping different bits of furniture with a simple rhythm. But this was perfect, amazing, and there was nothing that could make Atlas ungrateful for the shelter.

The first day was strange, and so different to anything Atlas expected - though he didn't know what he was expecting either. Eulalie was loud. He figured that out as soon as she collected him from off the street. She was loud, and seemed to have an enemy against pauses in conversations.

In the morning, she questioned Atlas about possibly everything; what happened, who is he with, how old is he, what's his last name. He stayed quiet for most of it, refusing eye contact and only offering basic information - information that didn't get him in trouble. She asked for his bag, in which he passed over hesitantly, feeling like a prison inmate.

"So.. Archie." she began. "Can I call you Arch instead? You don't look like an Archie."

Atlas shrugged. He wouldn't respond to either name.

"Okay, Arch it is," she sang, smiling so sweetly it made the boy's teeth hurt. Why was she so fucking happy?

She also made perfectly clear the rules of her apartment, setting them down in a two page list. The boy ignored the list, seeing 'no bringing round random people' as the top rule made him feel these really didn't apply to him at all. Eulalie stuck it onto her fridge, anyway.

"Just so you know, you can leave at any time. And I'm allowed to make you leave at any time. But to be fair, it's nice having someone around, having somebody to actually talk to." Eulalie said. "Don't worry, I won't kick you out. I'm supporting you through whatever you're going through."

Eulalie seemed really nice. Too nice. He didn't feel like he deserved her pitying looks she gave him, or the shelter she provided. *Why,* was the question. *Why* was she letting him live here, when he was giving her no money or things or gifts or whatever? Was she planning something? Or was she actually a nice person?

Another thing about her was that she never seemed to take the hint, even if Atlas hadn't said a singular word, she would ramble on and on about some random shit neither of them cared about. She also interrogated him like a Mother, trying to figure out what was going on. The boy just wasn't sure how to feel about it all -

but he knew, whatever it was, it was too much. For the first day in the new environment, whenever Eulalie went to the bathroom, or to her bedroom, Atlas broke down into tears. He was so confused, so lost, so depressed.

How did he even get here; why was he so fucking lucky?

Atlas knew that he should've been out on the pavement, freezing and lifeless as people scorned at him when they walked by. His brain urged him to run away from the woman, who was now in the kitchen, cooking a warm dinner for the two of them. She was evil, she was a witch, she was going to hurt him, his brain droned on and on.

The boy knew he didn't belong here. His plan was to go to fucking Brighton, and.. here he was, in some run-down, shitty apartment in East Worthing. Who even lived in East Worthing? What did it even have in it? From what he had seen, it felt like a deformed mix between the piers of Brighton and the danger of Bognor. No. No, he needed to get back on that train, to where he belonged, to Brighton. He didn't even know what he was going to do there. But he knew he didn't belong with Eulalie. He would only drag her down.

Atlas stared at the woman, who had her back turned, facing the pots and pans she was working with. He had to leave. The boy cautiously snatched back his bag which was draped over a hanger, and crept towards the door. He took a deep breath, silently, carefully, and grabbed hold of the handle. Pushing down gently, the boy's eyes widened.

It was fucking locked.

He tried again, less cautious this time, holding down and tugging at the door. Nothing. Completely.

Locked. Atlas turned around. Only to see Eulalie watching him with guilt and misery in her eyes.

"You want to leave?" she asked, slowly. Atlas said nothing. The woman walked over to where he stood so stiffly, and unlocked the door for him. "You can leave," she sighed. The wind pushed open the door, showing so clearly the boy's freedom. Right there. His brain shrieked at him, thoughts thrashing around, his muscles getting ready to run for it, away from the nice woman.

But he couldn't. Atlas looked up at the woman's face, and how pretty she was. Eulalie had vitiligo, her skin was so unique and perfect; golden tanned and white and brown and black, all at the same time. Her eyes shone brightly, revealing an unmistaken loneliness that she was battling, a clear depressive war inside her head. Just like the boy.

Atlas shook his head, and closed the door - locking it firmly. This would be good for him. A new place to stay. There weren't many angels like Eulalie in the world; he knew he was so much in luck to find her, or for her to find him. And it wasn't just for him, either. Eulalie was going through what he was, too. He wasn't alone. Atlas finally wasn't alone anymore.

Eulalie took a breath of relief, taking Atlas over to the dining table, telling him to wait there. She served up their food, some strange Italian dish he had never seen before, and then sat down with him. For the first time since Atlas getting there, it was completely silent. It was all quiet, but he could almost hear the words and questions and information she was trying not to spill out. Atlas was grateful for the silence.

The food was probably nice. He couldn't taste anything, it was all the same to him - but Eulalie seemed to be enjoying Atlas eat her food, so he carried on; much to the upset of his stomach. The boy hadn't eaten in days. He wondered what happened to the chips from Sadie, way earlier. Gods, it felt like weeks, months, since he had been at the Sunny Side Chips place, but it was only a day and a couple hours ago.

"I know you don't like talking but... I'm, like, here for you." she offered gently, holding out her hand towards the boy.

He smiled weakly, nodding at her. They both knew that there was no way the boy would "open up" to her, but *whatever*.

After the meal, Eulalie stood up to wash up the dishes, as Atlas made his way over to the bathroom. It was the same kind of style as the rest of the house - filled to the brim with plants and reminding the boy of a hippie hideout. It was almost obsessively clean, the sink sparkling so bright not even a fingerprints were visible. That was another thing about Eulalie -

everything in the house was meant to be somewhere, everything had a place. Atlas wasn't sure what his place was yet.

He sank to the floor, clutching the sides of the toilet bowl. He would have felt guilty for erasing the meal Eulalie made for him, but this.. this was probably his place. Atlas stuck his fingers down his mouth, gagging almost immediately - but nothing happened. He tried again and again, forcing them down further, but Eulalie's meal stayed stuck. He felt the panic at once like a repeating memory, but he shook it away.

It wasn't fair to her. She was doing so much for him.

Atlas heard a gentle rapping at the door.

"Archie? Everything okay in there?"

He jumped up fast, hitting his head on the sink, just as Eulalie walked into the room with him. The boy nodded at her, but she stared at him, confused.

"Were you.." she peered into the toilet bowl. Atlas shook his head.

Eulalie sat down on the tiled floor, up against the door - it made the room seem so much more suffocating and small. She smiled sadly at him, shaking her head.

"Have you got problems with food?" she asked. "I mean, like, it's okay if you do. I went through that phase ages ago but it wasn't for me. You don't need to be anorexic, you're way too skinny already."

Atlas stuffed his arms into his hoodie sleeves, looking down to the floor.

"Please don't throw up the stuff I make you. It costs me money and costs you your life." She waited for an answer, but the boy refused - looking guiltily away from her.

"Do you want a hug?"

"Yes.. please," Atlas croaked out. Tears threatened him as he shuffled awkwardly over to the woman, collapsing into her arms. She was so warm and full of love it felt impossible not to sink into her and cry.

The boy didn't know how long they were sat in the bathroom for, but it felt like way too long.

How did I get here, how did I get here, how did I get here?

8 -

Staying with Eulalie was going to take some time to get used to. Her apartment was cool, hippy-like, with spinning stars hanging from the ceiling to tapestries of art and ancient languages. Her apartment, number fourteen-B on the left hand side of the co-op, was full of colour; unlike any other house Atlas had lived in. It was small, really cramped, but everything was perfectly placed. It just.. worked. And it felt like a strange feeling of comfort.

Eulalie was extremely generous. She refused any sort of money for the shelter - not that Atlas had much to give anyway - and gave the boy gifts of coffee in the morning, flowers, and different clothes. She gave up her hot showers for Atlas to soak his aching bones in, and let him have first choice of whatever; whether that be food, or the television channel. She was great.

Her routine was pretty simple: wake up at five, go to the gym, make Atlas and herself breakfast, shower, go out for a couple hours, (Atlas assumed it was her workplace, but they hadn't talked about that yet), come back in the evening, make Atlas food, and go to sleep. On weekends it was almost exactly the same, except she came back drunk and almost always crying. It pained Atlas to deal with her after those nights, but it was the least he could do. In a way, this was his payment to her. The worst thing was, after he had cleaned up the sick, the blood, the bandages, and put Eulalie to bed, she would always forget about it in the morning. Maybe it was better to forget, but... but Atlas wanted her to know that he helped, in a way. He wanted her to know that he's trying, trying to pay her back in some way - or just to try and show her that he cares.

Maybe that wasn't even her routine. But it had been for the past week since Atlas had been staying with her. Altogether, his stay so far was okay - but awkward. He barely talked to her, so they mostly sat around doing nothing whilst Eulalie rambled on about something that nobody really cared about. She talked, and talked, then gave Atlas nice things that the boy knew he really didn't deserve - but the first time he had tried refusing something from his roommate (a new selection of expensive, urban clothes); she had gotten a bit offended.

"Oh," she said, over and over again. "I'm sorry. Do you, like, hate them? I thought you'd like them." Eulalie said, through sadness but annoyance too - speaking so quickly Atlas couldn't get a word in. After that, she placed the clothes on the sofa and quietly spoke: "I'm sorry it's not really good enough. I'm trying.", and walked off to her room without giving a chance for Atlas to go after her. The day after that happened, Atlas dressed up in the new clothes Eulalie bought him through shame, but presented himself to her with a small smile, and a 'sorry'. He didn't mean to seem ungrateful, he really wasn't at all!

He just didn't want so much money spent on him. So he learnt to accept Eulalie's lovely gifts.

Other than that, there were no fights, disagreements, or any malice. They watched movies together - all of which were Eulalie's suggestions -, ate meals together, and played board games. Maybe, just maybe, things were starting to get better. At meals, Eulalie always had a bottle of wine to go with whatever they had, but Atlas was refused whenever he eyed the bottles too eagerly. She even took away his bottle of vodka and packet of cigs, because she didn't want Atlas to 'go back to his habits', even though he had caught her slipping some of the alcohol into his lemonade one night. Atlas remembered sighing with relief when he realised his precious pocket knife hadn't been taken from him too. Eulalie really cared for him, like a mother - especially because of the fact that she was twenty five, but she didn't look it at all. Eulalie was kind of short, whilst Atlas was average -

tall - ish. Atlas tried smiling. She was like a fucked up young mother.

It was all such a massive change. He had gone from sleeping in parking lots, alone and miserable, to living in a flat with this woman. *Why him? When did this even all happen?*

Atlas woke up to the sound of a flat voice shrieking the words to 'Dancing Queen' by ABBA. He could have appreciated it, possibly even sang along if it wasn't five in the morning. Atlas wanted to show her that he was alive, happier, but his fatigue dragged him down into the snapped sofa. It was okay, though. He felt himself slowly getting more and more comfy with his beautiful roommate.

Eulalie skipped through the door, ignoring Atlas as he was usually asleep at this time, and slammed the door; going to the gym. The boy tried going back to sleep, but decided he could use this time to help with the chores as he normally did - even though Eulalie insisted he must rest and leave everything to her. Atlas made his 'bed', cleaned up the counters from the meal last night, and cleaned up some dishes. When Eulalie introduced Atlas to the apartment, he was shown all around - under the floorboard storage to the stationary boxes to where all the cutlery went. The day after he arrived, Atlas noticed all the knives had been hid away.

Eulalie was so sweet and caring it was almost sickly sometimes - but she only meant the best. She was so protective of Atlas, like a mix between an older sister and a security guard. The girl had told Atlas that he could go outside any time he liked, but as long as he gave her updates on his phone. Atlas didn't have a phone. The door was locked, and Eulalie always carried her key around with her, to the gym, to work, and wherever else she went. She promised to get another key fixed up soon, but for now Atlas was sort of stuck in the apartment. He kind of liked it that way.

It was his safety place. Nobody could get in. Or out. He was safe.

When the clock struck seven, Eulalie came back with wet hair and plastic bags from the co-op. Everyday, she made breakfast for them both; oats and fruit for her, and bacon and eggs for him. When he first came to stay, he told Eulalie that he didn't need breakfast, that it made him feel sick. She didn't listen, and told him that he needed to eat more. He ate his soggy eggs slowly, feeling his stomach churning with warning and tried hard not to breathe in the smell of bacon.

Today was Friday, so as Eulalie left for work, Atlas went to the bathroom and prepared some bandages for her. Just in case. It could've been a one time thing... but he wasn't taking any chances. Eulalie was so ram-packed full of conversations and problems that it felt like there was no room for Atlas' and he was enjoying it immensely, in a way. Because Atlas and Eulalie cared for each other, Atlas was preoccupied with her issues, so he didn't have to focus on his own. It was great, in a way.

But when she wasn't here.. That was more difficult. Atlas leaned over the toilet bowl, crouched over, on his knees. He felt so sick every morning because of Eulalie. She was trying so hard to make him feel better, but he always ended fucking it up somehow - first with the clothes, and now every single morning with his breakfast. Atlas reached into his throat carefully, and vomited up the food. He closed his eyes and reached for the flush.

When Eulalie left for work, Atlas had a lot of time to himself. Most days he stole back his cigarettes and smoked out the kitchen window, because he had hunted them down the second day back when he felt his hand jittering a bit too much. On the fourth day, he realised he was running out quickly - so he limited himself to half a cig a day. It seemed to be working. Other than planning how to ration out his addictions fairly, Atlas sat around all day and read the strange books Eulalie owned. Her whole room was basically a library - all coded in topics like romance to thrillers, scientific to narratives, fiction to factual. They all looked so interesting and powerful, but he could never finish a book. He found one, *'girl in pieces'*, which stuck out to him. The words in that book were dangerous. Atlas shut that book quickly, and placed it back where it belonged.

Eulalie's room was fascinating - her bed was massive, enough for three people at least, and all barricaded with books and clothes chucked on the floor. In the corner, there were plants and peeking out of one spider-plant, was a bong and a suspicious box. After that, he didn't go back in Eulalie's room.

As Atlas predicted, Eulalie came home a couple hours later under the influence. Where did she even get all this alcohol? With the amount of drinks she bought, the boy would have expected her to be put on a 'do not serve' list. Eulalie stumbled into the front room, kicking off her shoes and crying loudly. Atlas was sat awkwardly in a chair, watching her struggle to take off her coat. At least there wasn't any blood today, right? Did she even notice he was there? The obvious answer was no, when she started to take off her shirt and trousers too. Atlas quickly turned around, pretending to admire the wall, whilst he heard Eulalie running into her room.

He heard her sobbing into her pillow loudly for thirty minutes non-stop. What was he meant to even do? She was drunk, naked, and in her own bed. It was just wrong to go in there when she wasn't thinking straight. Which also meant Atlas couldn't comfort her, make sure she was safe, or okay.

"Archie.." she called out softly, her face obviously leaning into a pillow. "Archie, please come here." she cried.

What was he meant to do? Was this the right thing to do? He couldn't just leave her like that. But he couldn't go in and see her like that. It wasn't right. She wasn't thinking straight, Eulalie sober maybe wouldn't let Atlas see her - so why should drunk her? But at the same time..

"Archie.." she wailed again. It stung him to hear his friend begging for help. It sounded like she was in so much pain. But what could he do?

"Archie please.. I want to hurt myself. Please help me." Eulalie cried gently. He could only just hear the last sentence, and as soon as he made sense of it, he almost ran to the door. Atlas had seen her scars - and even though they weren't ever fatal, he never wanted Eulalie to do it again, to go deeper, to get *'braver'* with it. He wasn't risking her safety that night.

Atlas shoved open the door and flicked the lights on. There she was, smothered in blankets and pillows so there was just a lump in the bed sheets. His presence seemed to calm her down just a bit, her breathing slowing down and her cries becoming quieter. Atlas winced through his pain of trying to speak.

"Lee..? I'm here. I'm here for you." he whispered. Eulalie sighed with relief, but refused to move from her position.

"Can you.. uh- can you put some clothes on.." Atlas laughed awkwardly, even though he felt like doing anything but laughing right then. Eulalie nodded from her pillow, and got up to put on something. Atlas shot his eyes right down.

"I'm done." she croaked. Atlas looked back up again. She was wearing some pyjamas, and slumped on the edge of her bed. The boy sat down next to her.

"Um, are you.. okay?"

Eulalie sniffed, and flopped her head on his shoulder. Atlas wanted to shake her off, but it just wasn't the right moment. She needed comfort. What now? He never knew how to talk to people.. He didn't know what to say, what to do. Everything he could say would only make it worse.

"Why don't you... why don't you ever talk? Do you hate me?" Eulalie whispered.

"No. I don't hate you. I don't know why I don't talk. I'm sorry."

"Can I ...have a hug?" she asked hesitantly.

Atlas paused. "Uh.. yeah. Okay."

Eulalie pulled Atlas down onto her bed so he was facing upwards. She rested into him much to Atlas' discomfort, and went to sleep holding him tightly. She smelt like cigarettes, cheap beer, and vomit. Atlas hated it. He couldn't really move, he'd wake her up. Maybe she just needed someone to hold for the night. Atlas wished to himself that she'd forget all about this in the morning. It was embarrassing. And he didn't want her to do it next time. This was not turning into routine.

Atlas eventually fell asleep. Maybe it should have felt comforting, having another person curled up next to him - but all he felt was like somebody was going to hurt him. He wanted his own 'bed'. It just felt off, having somebody breathing next to him. It wasn't right. He kept waking up in between nightmares and dreams, before settling down again when he realised Eulalie was still latched onto him.

9 -

Atlas barely got any sleep, so when he woke up to Eulalie's slam of the door at five thirty, he was surprised. Somehow he missed Lee's wake-up call of an out-of-tune song, did he sleep through it or was she still miserable? He sat up slowly, remembering everything that happened last night. He noticed a new pot of beautiful flowers, marigolds, and a card addressed to him. The card read, with lots of smudges where she had stopped to think:

Hey Arch, sorry for last night. I was really drunk and I didn't think! I promise it won't happen again, it was completely my bad. I was gonna take a day off today n go to the beach wit u, but I'm not allowed. Sorry. Will see u at eleven, not coming back for breakfast. Here's some cash and the key to the front door (attached below!!!), if you lose it you owe me one, go get your own breakfast from the co-op. I'll know if u don't!!

Love u, soz again.

Atlas smiled at the letter and stuffed it in his pocket. He glanced at the ten quid Eulalie had given him and beamed even wider. It had been years since somebody had trusted him with money, let alone an actual note! And the keys - yeah, that was nice. The walls of the flat were starting to feel a bit suffocating so.. yeah. It would be good to get out for some air.

He pulled on one of Lee's jackets, lifted on the hood, and unlocked the door. Though he wasn't expecting beautiful, pure, fresh air - the powerful smell of cigarette smoke was abrupt. And a bit triggering, Atlas discovered as his hand started jittering by his side. He climbed down the outside steps to the flat, and walked into the co-op which was surprisingly cool and clean - unlike mostly everything else near Eulalie's flat.

The thought of being trusted with someone else's money had struck him with excitement with an intense desire to please Eulalie and spend it. But as he stared down at the aisles, his stomach churned nastily. He was *ill. Ill and broken.* He couldn't handle food at six - thirty in the morning. He'd just throw it back up, and waste Eulalie's money. Maybe he just wouldn't get anything, therefore breaking her trust. He wanted Eulalie to think he was better, and able to actually care for himself. He didn't think that he was doing a very good job proving that point.

"Can I help with anything, darling?" an old lady called out from the register. Atlas stared at her and shook his head, before disappearing into an aisle.

"This is so fucking stupid.." Atlas muttered, pacing up and down the food aisle. He felt a panic attack building up inside of him - and for what? For choosing a fucking meal? God, he was way more messed up than he had realised.

Atlas walked up to the self checkout, finally deciding on the cheapest, closest thing he could find from the entrance. He scanned them, and started flattening out the tenner to put it through the slot, when he identified that it was card only. Fuck. Now he'd have to talk to the old lady. Maybe she'd be nice?

"You got everything you wanted?" she smiled cheerfully, taking the two rectangular boxes from him. Atlas nodded. "Young man, that sandwich has mould on it." The old lady said. She looked up at him, and immediately froze. She stuttered, and took the food back. "You- um, excuse me. You can't buy that. It's out of, um, date." The lady kept scanning over his butchered face. Atlas felt so fucking disgusting.

For Gods' sake. I mean, what was he even expecting? Of course she'd see. And he needed food, but he felt his face burning with embarrassment, he knew he had to get out at once. What if she called the police on him? Eulalie knew the workers and she'd be told about him, surely. Then she'd be mad. Atlas left the food on the counter and walked out the shop in a hurry, ignoring the old lady telling him to wait. No food for him, then - there was no way he was going back in that shop. There'd be other shops. But.. he didn't know the area.

He trudged back up the apartment stairs in defeated exhaustion, slammed the door closed and locked it. Now he'd have to tell her he didn't get anything. And she'd be so annoyed with him. She'd be even more protective over him, because after all he was just some idiotic teenager that obviously couldn't look after himself.

Atlas walked over to the kitchen and got out a plate. He turned over the toaster to put crumbs on the plate, and left it on the counter. That was probably good enough. Next, he flipped over the carpet next to his bed, and retrieved half a cigarette. He lit it with a lighter in Lee's room that was next to the bong, and smoked it outside the window.

What now? He should probably give the money back, put it next to where the letter was and hope she didn't get mad. Atlas reached into his back pocket, but felt nothing. *Shit*, where was it? Did he loose it? *Fuck*. He felt the anxiety thundering again. Eulalie was gonna be so mad. She trusted him with money and he managed to fucking loose it. Maybe she'd kick him out. Or force him to make the money back. And how was he going to do that? Atlas turned out all his pockets, but nothing. Nothing. She was gonna be so mad.

All he could do until she came back was try not to worry about it. He had finally found somebody that liked him, that helped him and he had blown it. Yeah, it was only ten quid but it was still a lot. It was the thought too, if he didn't take care of one of Eulalie's possessions - what else wouldn't he care for? Her health? Her other gifts and important items? It took a lot for Atlas to focus on something else. He was so worried.

It was a Saturday, too. So whatever emotion she'd be feeling, the alcohol would make it about ten times worse. He had to man up. Lee had to know what he had done - otherwise she would find out through the old lady. And that would be even worse.

So when Eulalie came bursting through the door three hours later than expected, Atlas had prepared the bandages and a well-rehearsed apology. He had been waiting at the door since ten, making sure he got it all right, editing a few parts he thought wouldn't go down as well and speaking to himself in a nearby mirror. Lee looked down at Atlas, who was sat at the door, and brushed away a tear. There was blood trickling down her left arm. *Always* her left arm.

She wobbled uncertainly whilst helping Atlas up. She tilted her head, confused at Atlas' anxious face and tremble in his legs.

"Eulalie. I know you're drunk, but I have something to tell you and before I start, please know that it was a complete accident and I'll never do it again." he began. Eulalie sat down at the dining room.

"Go on." she spoke unnervingly.

"So I don't have the tenner you gave me and-"

"Oh." Eulalie interrupted. "Was it, like, not enough for your food?"

Atlas was taken aback. He didn't realise she'd take it like that. "No, no wait- that is not what I mean."

"Arch. Where is it?"

"No- listen, this is what I'm saying. I lost it-"

"So you've spent it on, like, what, drugs or something? And, like, the tenner wasn't enough for it?" she hiccupped. "Or you spent it on more cigs.

Yeah, I know about that. Why can't you just, like, talk to me or something? Are we not friends?"

"We are friends- and, and -"

"Doesn't, like, feel like it." she said, her voice raising. "You lost it. Arch, I get that you have forgetfulness, or, whatever's wrong with you.. but that was like two hours of my life. I won't really get that back." She shook her head and wiped her eyes again. "I'm too drunk for this shit. I'll talk to you in the morning. Sorry."

"Wait, no - don't apologise!" Atlas said, running after her as she slammed the door to her bedroom in his face.

Atlas wished she never drank. She was amazing when she wasn't - and sometimes she was great when drunk too, but.. she was just too much. It wasn't her fault, Atlas reminded himself. She was ill, like him. It wasn't her fault. She was trying to cope. Like him. His eyes flashed to the bandages waiting by the coffee table. Fuck. What if she did it again in her room? He grabbed them.

Atlas knocked against her door. He heard a small "come in", so he slid open the door and sat down on the floor. She was okay, thank fuck, but still sad. Her eyes were puffy and red and her makeup was running down her face. But, other than that. She was okay. Eulalie sat cross-legged on the edge of her bed with her sleeves up.

She sniffed helplessly, and asked Atlas to wrap up her arm. Does that mean she actually remembers all the nights he had done this before? Did she not ever want to mention them sober? It made sense; but he didn't want it to. He climbed onto the bed with her, and wrapped up her arm with the soft fabrics. He tucked it in neatly and smiled up at her broken face.

"Sorry for being such a cunt. Like, all the time." she laughed weakly.

"No, Lee-"

"No Arch, I'm being serious!" she exclaimed, dramatically slamming her hands down. "Like, how many times have I done this? I'm so sorry - I genuinely can't help it." she cried, her voice getting louder and louder.

"And.. and.. the worst part is," she sobbed, "is that, you're, like, completely sober. I'm sorry you have to, like, take care of me. It isn't fair. You're, like, thirteen-"

"Fifteen," Atlas said quickly.

"Fifteen," she repeated. "Fifteen. That's not fucking fair. I was probably playing with barbie dolls and that shit at fifteen. I'm sorry, Arch." Suddenly, she laughed, and shook her head. "No. No, that's a load of shit. At fifteen I had already been excluded twice and was trying every substance that was put in front of me. With barbie dolls."

"Me too," he quietly agreed. Eulalie looked up at him with her golden eyes. "Well - um. Only excluded once, actually. But, yeah." he stammered.

"Join me for a drink. Just a glass of wine. We can watch a shitty comedy, or a car crash compilation. I'll make your night interesting." she practically begged, holding onto Atlas' arm, but he shook her off.

"You wouldn't ask me to if you knew what I'm like." he sighed.

"What's that meant to mean?"

"Goodnight Lee."

Sleeping was hard that night. His body kept him up, tossing and agitated at the anxious want of the burn. The hurt. The feeling.

10 -

Atlas woke up to, thank God, Eulalie's singing voice stinging his ears. She was hustling around the house, searching for keys, clothes, money. She sounded happy.

"Archie, wake up. We're going out." she exclaimed. "Get changed, I want to be ready by twelve."

Twelve? She normally woke Atlas up at five? Did he sleep in..? He glanced up at the dining room clock, which read eleven. Why didn't she wake him up?

Eulalie pulled the covers of Atlas in a hurry, then wandered off to the bathroom. She was dressed up - not *fancy* fancy, but pretty cool-looking. She had a cropped flannel and a tight white tee, with brown cargos that had interesting pins and band patches. Atlas took that as he had to dress up too.

About half an hour later, he was ready. He chose what Eulalie bought him to be polite - a collared shirt with a woollen jumper over it. It didn't suit him at all. It looked weird, but not ugly - just not right. But it was okay. Lee liked it. Atlas made an effort to look for a mask, or something to hide his face; he didn't want people gaping at it wherever he was going; for Lee's sake. He didn't want to embarrass her. Much to his delight, he found a linen mask hanging in the bathroom cabinet, and put it on immediately.

They left at twelve exactly. Atlas pinched his nose when leaving the apartment to avoid the intrusive waft of cigar smoke nipping at his brain. Lee noticed this, but said nothing; hurrying Atlas along to the pavement.

Atlas didn't bother asking where they were going, he would have felt the same about it either way. Dull, nerve-wracking, and annoying. Plus, Eulalie loved to be full of mystery - it was exhausting, sometimes. She paced ahead of Atlas, five steps ahead, powerfully and with importance and every minute or so, looked behind her to check if he was still trailing behind.

"You look great, by the way. The style really suits you." she beamed. "I'm glad I chose it."

Atlas agreed with a "*mhm*," not wanting to sound rude. He felt a bit self obsessed, checking his appearance at every car window they passed. He looked weird and unlike himself, maybe that's why Lee liked it, cause who'd actually like him the how he is?

The two of them walked for about ten minutes to a restaurant. It was really fancy, with marble pillars and impressive architecture bordering the walls. Atlas' stomach churned. Was Eulalie taking him here to eat? He'd never be able to repay her, especially when he knew the lunch would end up being vomited up into the bathroom toilets. Eulalie noticed his shocked face, and pushed him playfully.

"We're not eating here, don't worry. I wouldn't spend *that* much on you," she laughed, walking up the stairs and through the doors. Atlas smiled genuinely, and followed, uncertain.

Inside was possibly even fancier than the outside. There were plants hanging perfectly from the ceiling, and Atlas noticed chandeliers sparkling up above. They looked like they were made from crystals, or diamonds. It was quite beautiful. There was a low buzz of chatter from customers, but other than that it was quiet and peaceful, and weirdly empty. Eulalie stood into an office area, so confidently that the boy instantly knew that she worked here.

Eulalie opened the door for Atlas, and pushed him inside, before following after him. The office was simple, with a wooden desk and comfy spinning chair. In the chair sat an old, balding man with a bow tie and black shirt. He looked Atlas up and down, and gestured for him to sit down.

"Good luck!" whispered Eulalie, before leaving the office swiftly.

Good luck? *Good luck for what?* Atlas looked around the office, instantly feeling the walls closing in on him. What was this place? Why did he need good luck?! Atlas felt his breath quickening, trying not to look at the older man.

"Don't worry, lad. Everyone's nervous for their first job interview."

Atlas calmed down at once. Just a job interview. Not some sketchy groomer-business that Lee tricked him into, just a job interview. Right, okay. The boy looked at the old man and nodded, more certainly. It made sense, too. He'd been living with Eulalie for a good couple of days, and she was probably sick of the rising water bills and extra food she'd have to buy. It would feel good to be doing something with his day, and finally being able to pay her back.

"So, you're applying for waiter role. I'm sure you know what it is, but I have to run it through just in case. Basically, you'll be taking orders, bringing food and drinks to table, and making polite conversations. Just before we start, you are paid by hourly rate, and tips do not go to you - they're shared between management. If you need a break, it comes out of your pay." the old man smiled. "We're like a family, so you'll love it here."

Atlas smiled with his eyes from under the mask. "Just one question," he said, trying to sound confident. "What's the pay?"

"Four quid an hour. Because you're under sixteen, we don't legally need to pay you anything over one pound, so four pounds is very good for a fine establishment like this."

It was better than nothing. It would just take longer to pay Eulalie back.

"Great. Can I just ask for you to take down your mask?" the old man smiled.

Atlas pulled it down, with hesitation. Great. This meant no job for him at all, he knew, as the bald man's pupil's widened, and his eyes showed concern. The man tensed up obviously, fiddling with his knuckled and scratching his mouth, perhaps wondering what it would feel like if he too had those scars. Surprisingly enough for the boy, he didn't call off the interview.

"Uh, okay. Er.." he continued, clearing his throat several times. "Well.. anyway, there's a few, uh, questions I need to ask., for safety." He paused to take a look at some notes he had made. "Have you ever been charged for any crimes?"

"No," Atlas lied.

"Any history of.. drug abuse?"

"No."

The man looked at his notes again, scribbling something down. "Okay, that's all the questions. Um.. why don't you take a seat outside?" he looked anxiously at the boy.

Atlas took a seat outside the office, slipping back on the mask. He shook his head to himself, knowing that the two questions that the manager had asked, he had lied to both. But it was fine. They were obviously desperate for a worker, otherwise the old man would have dismissed him the second he saw the scarred up face.

He looked around the restaurant again, trying to spot Eulalie - but she had disappeared. He wondered her role in this place, waitress, management, cook, or pot-wash? Judging by her confidence, Atlas would have said management, but.. yet again, this was Lee he was talking about. When wasn't she confident?

After five minutes, the old man called back Atlas into the room. He spoke quickly,

"You're a lovely guy, but.. you're just not what we're looking for."

"It's my face, isn't it?" Atlas snapped, atypical of his usual demeanour. The boy felt a strange amount of anger rising up in his blood. It wasn't his fault he looked like this! Except, it fucking was. Who else's fault would it be? It's not like some random person held him down and cut his face in two. This was him. And this was him suffering the consequences of being a dramatic brat.

"Do you want me to be honest?" the man said, matching the emotional reaction and clenching his fists together.

Atlas stood up from his chair, smacking it backwards onto the floor. "Be fucking honest, I dare you." Atlas saw the massive bullet he had dodged - just imagine working for this guy, he thought.

The man stared at him with newfound hatred. "Yes, it's your face. What am I meant to do, hire you at once even though you'll scare away all my customers? Get the fuck out of my sight!" he yelled, getting louder, louder, and angrier, angrier.

Atlas stormed out the stupid office, and slammed the stupid door, making sure to smack and kick any stupid object that was in his way. He pulled open the stupid fancy entrance door, and ran down the stupid marble steps. The worst part was, it was all his fault. All of it. He grasped the mask, and chucked it into a nearby puddle. If the world saw him as a freak, so fucking what? He didn't want the world. He didn't need it. He didn't need the stupid job. Didn't need stupid friends, food, shelter, water. He could just leave.

Eulalie was going to be furious with him.

Atlas wrenched open the apartment door and let it fall shut behind him. Eulalie wasn't in, luckily for him. He stared at the dining table, where two massive balloons stood tall and proud. At his place at the table was a bouquet of flowers, a chocolate bar and a card saying '*CONGRATULATIONS*', spelt terribly wrong - handmade.

The boy burst into tears.

Eulalie thought he was going to get the job, and he *failed*. She was so confident in putting her trust in him. And he had fucking destroyed his chances. *What the fuck was wrong with him?!* He crumpled to the floor, leaning against the chairs. He was such a fucking failure. She was going to be so angry - Lee had spent money and her precious time on him.

He *failed.*

Atlas pounded his head against the chairs behind him, again, and again, and again. He couldn't do anything right. The only thing he could do right was self sabotage. *Draw blood. Hurt himself.*

Turning away from where he sat, Atlas panicked when he saw red everywhere. His hair was falling out in chunks where it had been caught in the material, and his head felt as if it had been cracked in two. Now he'd have to clear this shit up, which was going to be difficult, since his entire world was spinning uncontrollably. He was such an idiot. Eulalie would kick him out. She'd be so disappointed. He couldn't stop the tears - they crept into his wounds and stung every time he twitched out of control. There was dark and sweet pain. The mix was bad. The mix was painful.

He stood up, and stabbed the balloons with a knife until they were lifeless, fallen, and dead. Atlas ripped the cards to shreds without reading the inside and resisted the urge to break into even more tears. The bar of chocolate lay untouched, in the middle. Was this a joke? Did Eulalie want him to become fucking disgusting? He had to get rid of it. Atlas opened up the bar, shoving parts of it forcefully down his throat, barely chewing. He ran to the toilet and spat it out, sticking his fingers down his throat to erase it. The taste was *sickening*. He was *sickening*. But he couldn't stop it. Atlas ate the rest of the bar, giving himself no time to breathe, before making himself sick again. The feeling was agonising. It was torture. But it was what he got, what he deserved.

He stared at the knife he had deflated the stupid balloons with, thoughts attacking his brain. No. Eulalie didn't deserve to deal with that. He had done to much. Fucked up far too badly already.

Atlas didn't deserve anything. He deserved nothing. And Eulalie was everything, she was everything. She was a sister he was so, carelessly, lovingly, deprived of. He wanted a sister again. He wanted his mother. But he knew he was so disgusting, so useless, so awful at being a human, so he didn't get one.

He sat desolate, alone, with vomit splattered across his new jumper and all around the bathroom. She was gonna be so mad. He lay in a puddle of his own blood, the smell of sick drifting in and out of his consciousness. She was going to be furious. He had no energy to get up or to clean the mess. She was gonna kill him.

Hours that felt like days past when Atlas finally heard the door being unlocked and opened, gently. He wished it was a burglar, or a hitman, armed with a gun to shoot him dead. But it was Eulalie, Atlas recognised by the way she called out her appearance. His stomach twisted with anxiety, threatening a death just like his sister's. The irony, oh, the irony.

As soon as Lee clocked what was going on, taking a glance at the deflated balloons and crimson blood pouring down onto the carpet; she rushed into the bathroom. The door was completely open, but she could've knocked it down anyway, in her stress.

"Archie?!" she screamed, "ARCHIE!", Eulalie shrieked in fear at the sight of him. Pale and skinny with blood seeping from his skull, ugly and deformed with sick mushed into his teeth. "Are you alive? Please, talk to me. Arch, please be alive, I love you so much."

Atlas tried hard to say something. but instead gasped suddenly. He started choking, inhaling a mix of bloody vomit and saliva. Eulalie grabbed his frail body and sat him upright, refusing to let him near a wall in case he started bashing his skull against it. "You can't fucking die. You can't."

This was so stupid. All over a fucking job interview. He already knew he was a fucking failure, why did he have to be so stupid and scary about it? But.. he hated seeing Eulalie love him. It scared him. Why, for fuck's sake, why did she give him so many nice things; flowers, cards, clothes, warmth, love? He deserved none of it. Worst of all, this was how he fucking repaid her?! No, that wasn't even the worst. The worst, most evil part of all of this, was that she wasn't even mad at him.

Eulalie sat upright against the wall, and almost cradled the small boy. She spoke strange poems in exquisite, outlandish languages and sung gentle rhythms until Atlas slowly, slowly, began to slip into a rest overcrowded with nightmares.

Eulalie wasn't mad at him. She sat by his side until the morning without sleeping. She didn't yell, hurt him, or even make any snide comments. Atlas expected to be kicked out at once, or for her to hit him, but.. no. Nothing. And that's what scared him most.

What was she planning? Or did she really, actually, properly forgive him?

His eyes drooped open, trying to make sense of his surroundings. Atlas was where he landed last evening - in Eulalie's arms. The sick and blood had been cleared up to perfection, but he didn't stir at all when Eulalie cleaned it all up. He must have been out cold.

"You're awake!" whispered Lee, trying to contain her excitement. "How are you feeling?"

Feeling that he may throw up if he opened his mouth, Atlas shook his head. The boy realised with discomfort that he had been changed out of his vomit-induced clothes and into some new, soft pyjamas. Eulalie caught his fearful look and rushed to explain;

"I had to change you out of your old clothes, Arch. They stank of sick and it grossed me out. Sorry if that wasn't okay, you weren't really able to say no or do it yourself, though," Eulalie's words fumbled out in a hurry.

She smiled gently at him, combing through Atlas' matted hair with her fingertips, stroking where he had bashed against the chairs the previous night, and Eulalie failed to see that every time she pressed against it, Atlas winced in pain. Or maybe she did realise, since every time the boy flinched in pain, she laughed to herself softly.

"Can we- can we get up?" Atlas smiled weakly. They had been sitting for about an hour, and Eulalie's hands near him weren't helping him get back to sleep for some reason. Eulalie grinned and pulled herself up, then insisted she had to carry him like a baby all the way to the dining table.

"You know, I'll never get used to how light you are, you skeleton," Eulalie jabbed him playfully in the ribs. Atlas stared down at his wrists, feeling his face go very red in embarrassment.

"What do you want for breakfast? I can make pancakes, bacon, toast-"

Her words mushed into each other and sounded more like another language rather than just her. His ears were ringing painfully, chucked full of blood from the night before. The ringing seemed to be getting louder, scratching into his flesh, burrowing into a hole-

"Arch? Cereal or bagel?" Cereal comes up easier.

"Cereal," the boy croaked.

Lee shook her head, her hair swaying behind her. "No, you need more than that. You just threw up all your energy, so you need something else." Atlas groaned to himself, slamming his head onto the table, hoping that would be enough to shut his fucking brain up. Food is food. Eulalie chuckled, turning her back to make him something.

The woman chatted at Atlas for about ten minutes about what she was doing today, who she was seeing, why she's not seeing her, why she likes her again, but it all went in one ear and out the other. She eventually shut up when she served Atlas' food, staring at him as if he was going to chuck it behind him, into the plant pot if she dared to blink.

He mumbled a 'thanks', and took a bite. It just felt like eating grey mush, he had no appetite for anything, but instead he chewed politely, staring intently into his lap.

Atlas felt Eulalie's eyes on him, it seemed like his stomach did too because in a second, he had thrown it all back up again onto the dining table - chunks of soft bread and a liquid, probably his body's acid dripping off the table.

"Oh- fuck!" Eulalie yelled. "Fuck! Archie, move, you'll mess up your clothes. Quick!" she shouted in a panic, jumping up at once to grab a paper towel.

Atlas limped away, over to the living room in a rush, taking a second to look back and see the destruction he had caused. For Gods' sake, why couldn't he just be normal for one second? He stood at the sofa, shaking hands by his sides, looking deathly and pale, feeling nothing but sorry for himself. Eulalie caught him staring, and cried out;

"Well don't just fucking stand there, help me out?!" chucking a cloth at him.

"But I thought you wanted-"

"Just help me out, obviously I need help!" she yelled. Atlas picked up the cloth and struggled back over to the table, scrubbing desperately at the sickness that had already begun to sink into the carpet, staining it a musty yellow.

They cleaned for twenty minutes in cold silence. Atlas sensed Lee's annoyance with him every time he gagged, coughed, or made any noise. He pushed down several instances of sick cramming its way out of his mouth, making him feel on the verge of passing out. The sick stained everything it touched, leaving mouldy looking patches in the table and the floor. How was that even possible?

Eulalie eventually threw down her cloth and sank to the floor. "This carpet cost me four hundred quid." she mumbled. "This table cost me a hundred and fifty." She leaned against the wall in defeat, and glanced at Atlas with anger in her eyes. "Well?"

"I'm sorry." Atlas rushed.

Lee shook her head, smiling furiously in disbelief.

"I'm sorry!" he pleaded. "It's just a stain, and I didn't do it on p-"

"It's just a stain?!" Eulalie repeated, standing up to face the boy. "It's just a stain! Okay, well, fine! It's just a stain!" she yelled manically. She stormed over to a painting nailed to the wall. "Fine! If my house doesn't fucking matter, then why do I even try?!" she bellowed, tugging it down, glass shattering everywhere, spilling to pieces across the carpet.

"Wait- Lee, what are you doing?" the boy whimpered. There he was, stood again, watching the destruction that he caused. He was such a disease, an infection, like a plague that hurt everyone around him.

"Well, obviously nothing fucking matters to you does it?! If I were to just kill myself you wouldn't even care, would you! Do you want to live in a fucking mess? You want me to die?!" she pushed over the dining room table, plates and vases of flowers crashing down in seconds.

Atlas closed his eyes for a second, begging to be taken away from this place, or just to collect his thoughts, calm her down, but this only angered her more. Eulalie screamed at him, chucking a shard of glass at him. It cut through his clothes in an instant, scraping past his skin then finally falling pathetically.

She saw the slit in the clothes and collapsed to the floor, tears staggering across her face.

"I'm so sorry.. I'm sorry, Archie. I'm so fucking sorry." she wept, over, and over, and over again.

What was he meant to do? Was she mad at him or not? Everything was fine one second, now half the kitchen was torn apart, battered, destroyed. All his fault.

"Archie," she muttered slowly, after a while of silence. "Archie. Under the sink cupboard, there's some vodka. Bring it to me, please."

Atlas went to the cupboard at once. He needed to get back on her good side. Not for him, no, not for his benefit. He couldn't bear to be hated by Eulalie. The thought of it sickened him. He grabbed the bottle immediately and gave it to her, sitting down next to her. The boy made a note to himself of where the bandages were.

The woman smiled at him sadly, yet gratefully. She took a huge swig of it, barely even grimacing at the burn. The burn that Atlas would kill for. The burn that his mind would kill itself for.

"I'm sorry," they both said at the same time.

"I'm sorry. I don't know why I'm the way I am," Eulalie sighed.

"I'm sorry I'm such a dick," Atlas sniffed.

"That's the fucking problem. You just piss me off all the time. I try so hard, Archie."

"I know, I know. I'm sorry. I'm ungrateful."

Eulalie nodded. She passed the bottle over to Atlas, "Here," she beckoned, "have some. Maybe I need you to be drunk right now." she laughed weakly. Atlas shook his head with what little self control he had left. He couldn't. Shouldn't. He'd get kicked out. Eulalie shoved the bottle into Atlas' hands.

"Like I said," she rolled her eyes, bitterly, "Ungrateful. I'm not taking no for an answer. Think of it for me, not for you. I can't deal with you right now."

"I'll just be worse when drunk," Atlas pleaded. This was how he was going to get kicked out. He was calling it now. Eulalie would regret it.

Eulalie took another gulp of the liquid, repulsing only slightly at the metallic taste. Suddenly, her face broke out of annoyance and into fits of quiet laughter. "Archie, you can tell me that you've never drank before. I don't judge."

"That's not what I'm saying, Lee. I don't want to be drunk."

"No, I get it, I was scared my first time too!" she giggled, pouring a shot into the lid and shoving it into his hands. "Here, just.. just drink it and you'll be fine."

The boy sighed, and drank it without complaining this time. Lee could believe whatever she wanted, if it made her happy; it made her happy. The slow slip of the drink gliding down his throat felt like an awoken heaven to him. The liquid fire burnt like a cigarette, turning and twisting comfortably, down, and down. But after that, the burn stopped. His mind yearned for more, for the feeling. He urged himself, no, but Eulalie kept smiling and pouring him glass and shot after glass and shot.

Atlas could have said no. He didn't want to, though.

Soon, they were both sleepy and dazed out of reality. Atlas was glad to realise Eulalie was a quiet drunk, and instead of her bouncing around the walls screaming at the top of her lungs, they were both sat against the counters, talking strange conversations that neither of them would have even thought of whilst sober.

The bottles never seemed to run out. Every thirty or so minutes, Lee would stumble back over to the cupboard under the sink, or behind the microwave, or even hidden between two books to get more spirits or wines or whatevers. Atlas lay back with his head up, smiling properly for the first time in what felt like months. In fact, how long had he even been here? There was no calendar, no phone, and he had no care to ask Lee the date. He shook his head, begging himself to not start thinking.

Staring up at the ceiling, Atlas grabbed the bottle that Lee had brought over. He was too wobbly and pissed to pour out anything - they were way past that now, anyway. Eulalie laughed at him as he flooded his throat with the angelic burn.

Atlas' brain felt like it was flooding over, his sentences and thoughts mushing and sinking to the bottom where they belonged. This, this is what he wanted. Not feeling real or present without reasoning was so fucking boring. This new fuzziness, the blurred .. blurred everything was good. It was so great. And he was normal, too. Everyone pissed stumbled when they walked. Everyone pissed couldn't talk for shit. Everyone pissed was in pain. He was so normal drunk.

"You," Lee pressed her finger into Atlas, leaning into him - personal space didn't exist when shitfaced. "You were completely..." she paused, staring into his eyes, mouth wide open. She reminded him a bit like a goldfish. "Completely.. wrong. Yeah. Yeah, you're like, um, so cool when you're drunk, Arch." Eulalie blushed.

Atlas gazed into her eyes. How could someone have such saturated eyes? How were they so golden? He wanted to pick them out, carve them out.. *carve*? *Carve*. Such a good word. *Carve*. What's been *carved*? A *carvery*? *Carved*. *Carve*-y. Harvey. *Carve*. The boy blinked slowly, eyes dropping. Nothing made sense, and that all made sense to him. Does that make sense? *Carve*.

"Stop staring at me, weirdo." she pushed him away with a grin. "I love seeing you like this, you know? Like.. you're happy. I don't like seeing you sad. Makes me sad. I love seeing you so absent. Like, I could do anything to you and you'd just accept it."

The boy looked back down in his lap in a hurry. He wanted to say so badly that he loved seeing Eulalie like this, too. But words fumbled around in his brain, it seemed impossible. He wanted to say how much he loved her like his sister, how much he just needed a hug. He wanted his sister back.

Stop thinking. Stop, fucking, thinking. *Carve*. It's a weird word. Two.. uh, what are they called.. Vowels. Two vowels for a, what, five letter word. Atlas awed at it. No more thinking. Distract. *Distract. Carve.*

"I am, like, officially an alcoholic," Eulalie chuckled, pointing to the clock. It was only four in the afternoon, and they had finished two bottles of white wine, a bottle of sourz, which Atlas refused to drink anymore of, and the vodka bottle was halfway finished.

"We deserve it," Atlas said.

She nodded, pulling the boy up. "I'm, like, tired and that. I want to go to bed."

"Can I just finish off the bottle myself-"

"No.. no, definitely not. You're like twelve. Twelve year olds can't drink." Lee walked off, going to her room.

"Fifteen. I'm fifteen. Will you be okay tonight?"

Eulalie stopped in her tracks, her shoulders slouching in a bit. She sighed, and whispered; "I guess we'll find out." She walked into her room, and shut the door.

Atlas groaned to himself quietly, working his way around the shattered glass with what little balance he had left, and into Lee's room. He knocked twice but entered anyway, not bothering to wait for her response. The boy collapsed onto her bed.

"I'm getting changed. I don't mind if you, like, look." Eulalie yawned from the other side of the room.

The boy closed his eyes, tight. He could feel the hangover creeping up on him already. Atlas was dreading the next day. The glass was still on the floor in the dining room. The painting was smashed up. His sick was still mushed into the table and carpet. And Eulalie... well, he was here, right? He could prevent her by sleeping in the same room, prevent her from carving into her.. *Carve*. That's where it's from. *Carve*. Into skin.

"Hey, I was joking! Don't look, you creep." she stumbled whilst changing into her bottoms, crashing to the floor in a rush.

"I wasn't." Atlas said, quickly.

"Yeah, I thought so. I wasn't looking to see if you were looking to see if- oh, whatever." she slurred. "I wanted to see if you looked."

"That'd be weird." the boy drawled, his words slipping up on each other. Talking was so difficult. At least he had an excuse. It would all be over soon.

"Yeah. Weird. Aren't you going to, like, change?"

Atlas shook his head, blood pounding from ear to ear. "No. No, I have pyjamas on already."

Eulalie threw the cover over them, and turned around to sleep the upcoming hangover away. It was strange being in somebody else's bed for the night. It was strange hearing somebody else's breath gently exhale, inhale, exhale, inhale... He loved the pattern of her breath. It was also strange feeling so warm in the night. Her body heat was like a mother's, cradling a small infant. Atlas got to sleep fast, for the first time in a long fucking time.

12 -

The next two weeks passed in a hurry. Their hangovers passed and they helped each other clean up all the mess from the night before. Things really seemed to be calming down - sure, there were a few arguments here and there, but Eulalie's little apartment quickly became feeling like a home. Lee didn't bother finding Atlas another job; she said she didn't want to 'stress him out'. *Whatever.*

He'd begun sleeping in Eulalie's bed. Not in a weird way. In a way where if he didn't, he felt scared for her. Plus, his makeshift bed in the living room made his back ache - and the warmth of another person there was nice. It really was. She woke him up at five, every morning, just like normal, and they had started to make breakfast and run errands together, which Atlas appreciated. It felt like he wasn't just stealing from her, finally.

Today was a special day - and Eulalie had made it clear very loudly for the past four days. She was turning twenty-six. Apparently that was a big deal. They weren't doing much that day - Eulalie told Atlas she didn't expect him to do anything for her. He planned something, anyway, but something that didn't cost anything.

Atlas had set an alarm stuffed under his own pillow for four in the morning, so it would only wake himself up. Today was going to be good. Maybe even their best day together yet! The boy swore to himself to not piss off his friend at all today. It was her special day, all about her.

Atlas sat up, and rushed to stop the alarm. Eulalie lay next to him, facing the window - stealing the entire cover. She looked so peaceful asleep. Like nothing was actually wrong, ever. He wished she could be like that forever. He got dressed, quickly, then tip toed over to the kitchen. The boy grabbed flour, milk, sugar, and eggs. He liked knowing where everything was, feeling like he was in control. He could control where the sugar lived, and it was in the top left cupboard. Things were getting better.

It took him about six times longer to prepare the batter than the recipe told him - and about three times that to clean it all up again. He felt exhausted at his efforts, but stared proudly into the oven where the birthday cake was rising, just like the book had told him it would. Eulalie was going to be so happy with him. Atlas had never baked before, but it was proving to be quite therapeutic. Especially when it went so well - even if it was time consuming. Just as he was taking the cake out the oven, he heard a sudden outburst of ABBA playing from what he could only assume was Eulalie's phone. Five o'clock.

"What's that?" Eulalie exclaimed, even stopping her 'Winner Takes It All'.

"Nothing, don't look!" Atlas smiled, half attempting to hide the tin behind his back, but the boiling tin rubbed against his fingers and burnt him quickly, so he crashed it down onto the counter in an instant. "Oops".

"You made me a cake," Eulalie paused.

Atlas froze. "Um.. is that okay?"

She laughed and ran over to him, hugging the boy tightly. When she pulled away, she grabbed Atlas' shoulders in excitement. "Yes! Yes, it's okay. I just wasn't expecting it. Thank you so much."

Atlas was very pleased with himself, holding his head high as Eulalie walked out the house for her usual run. Now.. did he risk putting icing on it too? Or was the sponge on its own enough..? Maybe the risk was worth it, he decided, and got to work.

The boy gazed at the cake a good thirty minutes later. It was probably the most amazing thing he had ever made. Two tiers of vanilla sponge with yellow buttercream. It was partly lopsided to the left, and the icing was blotchy and pulled apart the back of the cake, and on the top, he had already starting picking of the iced gems he stuck on there. If you just squinted.. then closed your eyes, then imagined a perfect cake, it was perfect.

He presented it to Eulalie with an acapella, very out of tune 'Happy Birthday' song when she came back from her run. Atlas even dimmed the lights, and used his hand as a pretend candle, wiggling it about on the unlit wax - all the lighters had been hidden away a long time ago, since Lee finding Atlas' cigs. Eulalie enjoyed herself immensely through the entire thing, blushing deeply and laughing at Atlas' out of tune rendition of the song. They sat at the table and ate the cake with wine glasses, digging it into the cake and then using their fingers to pick it out.

"I never expected this, I can't thank you enough Archie." she choked out through laughter. Atlas grinned at her, and kept picking at the cake. It was okay, definitely not as good as Lenore's.. but it was okay. He pushed it all down, ignoring the feeling of guilt struggling about in his stomach. Not on her birthday.

"You can now officially, legally, do nothing new," Atlas smiled. "And adopt a child."

"I should legally adopt you then." Eulalie stuck her tongue out at him. "Literal child."

"I'm fifteen." Atlas grumbled.

Eulalie took out her phone, and typed in a couple words. "I could adopt you, like, legally."

The boy tensed immediately. She knew nothing about his parents. He had told her nothing.

She giggled at him, and grabbed the now empty glasses, taking them to the sink. Atlas jumped up immediately to help her, taking a cloth and drowning it in washing up liquid. They chatted happily together about what was going on today - Atlas found out that she was going out with her friends in the evening.

"You can't come. They're, like.. weird." she stopped to glance at him. "Weirder then you."

"Are they druggies or something?"

Eulalie snorted, "Obviously. But they're just kinda dickheads. Especially for people like you."

"What does that mean?"

She took a look at Atlas' offended glare, and said in a hurry; "Nothing personal. Just think basic school chav." Atlas shrugged, and scrubbed at the tin.

For the rest of the morning and part of the afternoon, they watched two movies Eulalie had pirated from some guy. They watched 'Fight Club' and 'Wild Child'. Atlas loved the first movie so much more, watching the men crash into the floor and beat each other felt so satisfying. He sank into the ending music, letting 'The Pixies' flow through his ears. It was amazing. After the movie, Eulalie put on about three hours worth of theory videos on who was real and who wasn't - at the end of them Atlas was even more confused than he was before.

Wild Child was less interesting - but apparently a 'must watch', according to Eulalie and all her friends. He zoned out for most the movie, thinking more about the other one that intrigued him so much more. He pictured himself at the table, with the man with those sunglasses, and him pouring the chemical burn onto his hand. It burnt into his skin, seeping through the layers like a plague. The scorch licked at him painfully, holding him still yet feeling his bones shaking and rattling in fear, begging to be-

"You okay?"

"Yeah, sorry. Zoned out."

Eulalie rolled over from her spot on the sofa, and turned to face him. "I like that you talk more now. Like, in my eyes, it means you're more .. like.. comfortable with me."

The truth was his scars across his mouth were healing, slowly, yet surely. It still pricked at his skin whenever he opened his mouth to talk, but it was better than the constant feeling of a knife being plunged past his gums. But at the same time, he supposed she was right. Atlas was never very talkative, because nobody wanted to hear what he had to say. Maybe his brain was subconsciously realising that Eulalie wanted to hear him, and he wanted to be heard again.

"Don't go all quiet on me again, I put up with that for weeks," she chuckled. "God, I remember how mucky you were when I picked you up from that street." She shivered almost comically. "I'm so glad I found you. You're so fun."

After Wild Child, they played old board games that had a thick layer of dust cemented on all of them. The woman explained that nobody ever wanted to play them with her, but now she had Atlas to win against. And she was right; she won monopoly, go for broke, and a weird family game called the 'Game of Life'. When they passed the marriage section of the game (much to Atlas' hatred), Atlas was surprised to see her pick up a blue character - a husband.

She met his eyes, and cocked her head. "You thought I was *gay*?" she laughed. "I mean, that lifestyle is fine, don't get me wrong. But absolutely not." She paused, then gasped in shock. "Oh my god. Do I, like, look like a lesbian? Is that why men aren't chatting me up?"

Personally, Atlas thought it was more of her loud personality and the fading scars climbing up her arm like a ladder. He could just never see her with a man. She was far too bossy and intimidating for a guy to be interested.

Atlas landed on the marriage icon, and stopped over the little pink and blue plastic mini figures. Eulalie leaned over too, clearly interested on his choice.

"What about you, then? Boys or girls? Or both.." Eulalie said, giggling. His hand hovered over the mini figures. Why did he feel so much pressure? It was just a game.

"Come oonn.." Eulalie droned on. "Just tell me. I won't judge." Atlas withdrew his hand, making Eulalie shoot him a questioning look.

"I pick neither," Atlas said. It didn't feel right.

"You don't like girls or boys?"

"I don't want to date, ever. That's not me."

Eulalie took a second, before speaking; "So you like nobody?", to which Atlas nodded. She shook her head, smiling. "No, you just haven't met the one yet. And you're only twelve, you're too young to know if you like sex or not."

"Fifteen."

"Then you just haven't met someone who has made you feel like that, yet. God, be glad I picked you up, I'm like your relationship guide!"

"I don't like sex."

"You've never tried it though!" she exclaimed, then squinted at Atlas, asking the question in her head. Atlas shook his head no at once. "See? You need someone to show you!" She slowly winked at him.

"Gross."

Eulalie grinned, telling him he'd get used to it. They carried on playing the game - Atlas ended up winning but Lee told him that it didn't count, he broke the rules and didn't have a stupid pink or blue plastic figure, so she won instead.

They played mindless games for a bit longer, talking about random things that entertained the two for a while. Eulalie stopped to make food before she went out, and Atlas got up to help her. They ate happily, Atlas singing 'Happy Birthday' again when he brought the cake out for afters. Then, Eulalie left to see her friends. Atlas was left to himself, probably for the rest of the evening and the night. A walk would have been nice, but Lee made it clear she didn't want him going out without her.

Atlas washed up the dishes by himself. It wasn't as fun with Eulalie, but that was to be expected. The boy wandered around the apartment several times over out of boredom, rediscovering cool things in the apartment he had overlooked before. He tried playing monopoly by himself but kept loosing, so he gave up. Atlas ended up re-watching 'Fight Club' again, letting himself be absorbed into the strange movie.

Like he predicted, Lee came back very late. His eyes checked on her as she came bursting through the door, checking for any blood or wounds. But no, everything was okay. However, there was something else..

In her hand, she carried her keys, and a bottle of beer - as usual. However, in her other hand, pinched beside her two fingers was a blunt. It stank out the entire apartment as she entered, taking in a long drag, then exhaling it carelessly into the little flat. The smell activated Atlas' fight or flight, his panic rising by the second.

"Lee? Could you take that outside?" he asked politely, but the woman refused. Eulalie smiled, and walked into her room.

He sighed roughly. That smell.. it took him back to the alleyway with the boys. He didn't know why - it was fucking annoying. It was just weed. Weed! Why did that memory make him so worried? So much worse had happened before. When he smashed up the entire IT room to get Richard not to tell anyone, as some sort of failed threat, he had been held down by two of the school counsellors. They pushed him down, and pressed their knees into his chest so he couldn't move. One of them even smacked his hand when he tried fidgeting away. That was worse. Why didn't he care about that? Why the *weed*?

The boy took a deep breath, and stepped into Lee's room. It immediately wafted around him, submerging him into a state of invisible fear. He calmly walked up to Eulalie, who was sat on the windowsill, smoking the blunt slowly, clearly making it last. He hoped this wasn't a regular thing.

"Want to try some? It really calms you down." she said, yawning, and holding it out to him. It was nearly all out. Though his stomach was doing flips and his anxiety was making his hand shake uncontrollably, he took the blunt. Maybe all he had to do was get used to it. He couldn't just be scared of a scent for the rest of his life.

Atlas blocked out Lee trying to explain how to inhale - how innocent did she think he was? Then, took a long drag of it. At first, he felt paralysed in terror. His brain screamed, urging him to throw up - the bad scent was inside him. It was going to bring back the boys. But then.. he felt his body melt into the fumes, and his mind being barricaded over with clouds.

After only ten or so minutes, Atlas felt as if his mind was zoomed out backwards several miles. He sat patiently, docile in his head, watching the world go by - very fucking slowly. He kept losing focus; drifting in and out of a paralysing dream-like state. The edges around his brain blacked out and fuzzed, dissolving round and round like particles fighting each other. Atlas couldn't tell if he liked it or not, or if he was terrified of it. Maybe a bit of both.

They shared what was left of the weed, and headed off to sleep. Atlas slept well. He was sleeping so well recently. It was all getting better.

13 -

Winter was approaching, fast. The boy found himself most days staring at the dark black sky at seven in the morning with a sense of coldness pulling at his heart, watching the leaves on the trees grow rigid and glide off gracefully, down to the grainy pavement. Every night the days got shorter, and shorter - leaving only space for shitty movies and sleep.

He hated winter. It was freezing, wet, and miserable, and it never even snowed like it was meant to in those movies Eulalie had made them start watching. The breeze of the wind and the darker evenings made Atlas feel just a bit sadder, but it was okay, Eulalie was there with him.

One thing he did like was all the Christmas baking they were doing. Eulalie brought home ingredients for cakes and gingerbread house kits, which ended in disaster - the pieces of gingerbread was still scattered around the kitchen after it had been smashed with a cricket bat Lee had found. November rolled around and the entire apartment was decorated head to toe in silly ornaments and paper loops, green and red and white. Atlas put his foot down when Lee tried pulling up the Christmas tree in October.

"It's not even Halloween! Don't you celebrate Halloween?" laughed Atlas, sitting on the box Lee was trying to pull out.

She shoved him off playfully, making him land uncertainly on the carpet; which had silver glitter left over from Christmases years ago.

"No, Halloween is for the Americans. Plus, you don't know what those people are handing out. I got a razor in my lolly one year."

Atlas turned away with a smile, mumbling that she probably was happier with *that* rather than getting the candy. This earnt the boy a smack round the head with a newspaper. They both giggled together.

Things were definitely going great. When they were together, Atlas' life felt full. They had so much to do; like watch shitty movies recommended by Eulalie, cook new meals together, do house chores, play games, and make cupcakes and cookies. But when Lee went away, Atlas didn't know what to do with himself. When Lee went away, the apartment felt so big. When Lee went away, Atlas felt fucking depressed.

It was kind of pathetic, how different he felt when she was gone. When she left, it was like she took Atlas' heart along with herself. The boy thought over and over about how fucking lame he was. It's not like she would be gone for ages, anyway; the most Lee had been away for was about three days, and she never explained why - Atlas learnt not to ask.

So when Eulalie announced she was going out, Atlas felt a boulder drop in his stomach. He couldn't help feeling anxious whenever she left; what if she left for good? What if he was taken away when the neighbours called the police, seeing nobody leave the house for months?

That was another thing. Atlas never left the flat. He didn't want to; the world outside was cold and scary and boring and gross. And that suited Lee, who said she didn't even want him going out anymore. The world was '*too dangerous*' for him. Whatever the fuck that meant.

He had started talking so much more, even like a normal person again. The pain had almost vanished, though his scars were still red and sometimes bloody when he picked at them. They were still carved into him and the scabs stuck out randomly - he wondered if he'd ever *not* have them. He felt so much happier with his friend, Lee. He felt so confident talking to her, he felt like he was talking to Lenore again. It was so comforting, like a blanket of words cosying into him.

They still fought. They still argued. Eulalie still yelled. But it was becoming less. The amount of times Eulalie would walk through that door with blood dripping down her arm was becoming less, and less, and less. But it still happened. Lee was allowed to have bad days.. it was just difficult to deal with them.

Eulalie returned from wherever she went about seven and a half hours later - not that Atlas was counting. In fact, when she went away, the boy stared at the clock in the kitchen like a dog waiting for its owner. Time ticked so slowly without her. But whatever, Lee was never going to know about that.

She came through the door, and Atlas immediately recognised something was very wrong. Her eyes were red and puffy, and there was a single tear dripping down her cheek. He scanned her arms in a flash.

Blood. Thin, red blood, oozing out her skin and *drip, drip*, dripping down onto the floorboards. She'd gone deeper this time, Atlas could tell by the way she held herself it stung badly, how her teeth clenched together as the wound brushed against her coat, how her dermis was plunged into, spilling out gushes of crimson blood. Her arm looked so much worse than usual, the small scratches that had lay there before were now slashed at - leaving only thick ladders of cuts leading up, and up, until Atlas couldn't see them anymore. How far did they go up to?

He should have felt sick at the sight of the wounds. He should have shuddered at the thought of Lee slitting her skin in two, pulling apart what held her together, sat in a bathroom stall, cut, after cut. But, no. His fingertips fidgeted at the thought, hands shaking at the want of a blade for himself. His mind sped disgusting thoughts that he should have repulsed at, but it only drew him in further.

Her wounds were so beautiful. So evenly placed, each one, so perfect, all with different layers of deepness, he could tell she gradually got riskier with each cut, until finally, the last one wasn't even bleeding. It was white.

Atlas shook himself back. *What the fuck was he doing?* Eulalie went too far - she could be in danger, and here he was, fucking admiring the lovely, no, the sickening lines. What kind of a friend was he?!

"Are you okay? What's wrong?" Atlas rushed over to the door.

Eulalie held a crumpled piece of paper in her fist. She glared at Atlas with fury in her eyes, then tossed the paper at him. The boy stared at her in fear - what was he meant to do?

"Fucking read it then!" she yelled furiously.

He took the paper, and carefully uncrumpled it, making sure not to rip anything, but his shaking hands was proving to make it a very difficult task.

"When were you going to tell me, Archie?!" Eulalie screamed. "Or should I say, *Atlas*?!"

Atlas' heart skipped a beat. There he was, centred on the page, labelled as a "Missing Child". He looked at the paper quickly, feeling the walls around him grow smaller, and smaller. His eyes flicked nervously over the paper - seeing that his parents had offered no reward, only their own number, and the police.

Fuck.

He looked up from the paper, dreading to meet his friends eyes. Eulalie snatched back the paper, and threw it to the ground. Her arms were bloody and covered from head to toe. He needed to sort her out, quickly, she was loosing blood fast, quickly.

"They're not even offering a reward. Don't worry, I made sure to check." she grimaced with fury. Atlas started to reason with her, when she yelled; "Don't you fucking dare talk to me. Who even are you?!" She shoved him out the way, and stormed to the bathroom, locking it furiously behind her.

Atlas had lost his voice, once again. It had been stolen away by her arms, capturing it like some tortured soul. He stood, frozen, paralysed in terror, between the lounge and the door of the bathroom. He heard her gasping for breath through her teeth over and over and over and over. He knew what she was doing.

The boy banged on the door so hard it would've broken if he wasn't so fucking weak. He heard her sharp intake of air repeating on and on and on and on in his head, he didn't even know what was real or not.

"Eulalie," he croaked.

"Don't fucking talk to me- shit, *ouch*!" she shouted in pain.

"Please, stop."

"This is all your fucking fault. I might even *die*. Because of *you*."

Atlas collapsed to the floor, right at the bathroom door. The boy sank to his knees, crumbling down in a pitiful heap, leaning fully into the door. They were right next to each other. He was right next to his friend, blocked by a fucking door, sobbing at every yelp of pain she groaned out. He clung onto the doorframe, begging from some sort of stability from the world which was spinning uncontrollably. Or was that just him?

It should have been him. *It should have been him, not her*. Lee didn't deserved pain. She was the best thing that ever happened to him. Eulalie gave him love, food, and shelter - and what did he fucking do to repay her? The boy had lied and cheated her out of who he really was. He was disgusting. He was killing her - he was killing everyone around him like a disease. Atlas deserved everything bad that Eulalie did to him.

"*Please*," he begged, crawling as close as he could, like a fucking dog. "Please," he begged, tears spilling down his face and choking his words as they came out. He spat at the floor, pleading to be heard - but his voice was gone. He was back to the hollow vessel he was three months ago.

He curled up into a ball, cradling himself; though he knew he didn't deserve comfort. He was murdering her. He was killing her, day by day, pissing her off, and making her cut up her arms. It was all his fault.

On and on, he kept repeating and repeating unheard words, crying for forgiveness, for Lee to stop, *please, for fuck's sake, stop it, stop it, he had learnt his lesson, please.*

The door swung open, crushing into the pathetic boy. The wood smacked him to the side, making him land on his side with a thud. His ribs ached almost immediately, hugging him tighter, and tighter, and tighter, until he could barely breathe. The apartment was getting darker. The apartment was getting blurrier. Everything was shaking.

"You fucking dare pass out now? Look what you've done." She screamed, forcing Atlas into her and holding out her wrists. She had cut herself into tiny pieces, all jagged and ugly. She wanted to do it until there was nothing left of her arms - but she wasn't brave enough. Basic, shallow, boring fucking cuts. Blood poured out from her scratches, spilling out, down to her fingers which smelt of rusting metal.

Atlas grabbed her arms, wanting to get lost in them. The liquid drip of her warm blood made him stop and gaze at the scars. It was so real. It was so.. *perfect. So neat. I did this, I did this. This was me. It was mine.*

Lee pulled her wrists away, and slapped the boy's cheek. "What the fuck are you doing, drooling over my-" she paused suddenly, her mouth dropping.

"Oh my god," she said, pacing up and down the corridor. "Oh my god!" she laughed, clutching her head, blood spilling over her hair. "You get off to this shit, don't you?!" she shrieked, grasping Atlas' collar.

"No, what the fuck?! I swear, I don't!" he yelled back, for the first time, ever.

Eulalie held him tighter. "Archie! No, fuck, Atlas." she scowled, anger building up faster. "Atlas," she mocked his name, letting it roll off her tongue. "No wonder you forced me to cut myself. No wonder you drove me to this. You can't fucking get enough of it, can you?!"

Atlas wept, out of control, his blood pulsing against his chest, urging to be released.

"*Please-* believe me!"

She threw him to the floor, almost too easily. "I'm going to bed. You're fucking *disgusting*."

Atlas stared at the woman passing by him, longingly. He just wanted to be loved. He wanted his sister back. His Lenore. He wanted his Mother. Why did he always have to mess it up? He wasn't a creep. His addiction just crept up on him, like a spider, creating dangerous webs over all his relationships; trapping them and causing destruction. He reached out to her, attempting to clutch onto her leg or something.

He didn't know how low he stayed down on the floor for, but he knew, however long, it should have been more. He was less than an animal.

It took a while for the boy to drag himself back up, always failing with him collapsing back down again. Every time he got up, it was like then Gods were pushing him back down, where he belonged, where he should have stayed. Nothing more than a filthy mutt.

Atlas dragged himself across the floor, his ribs crushing into each other. Everything was stiff. Everything hurt. He wished it hurt more. He wished it burnt.

The boy tapped at Eulalie's door. To his surprise, she let him in after ten minutes. She lifted Atlas onto the bed, and scowled at him.

"I know I fucked up-"

"Just a bit," Lee scorned, refusing to meet his eyes.

Atlas climbed up close to her. "I don't get off to that." he said. Eulalie rolled her eyes.

"You're so boring," she snapped, pushing him away again.

"So you want me to fucking like you cutting yourself? What the fuck are you saying?" Atlas cried.

"You're such a yes-man."

"So you'd prefer me to... to like *that*?!" The boy felt his temper rising with the woman, pointing to her bandaged up wrists.

"Why are you yelling at me?! Haven't you done enough?" Eulalie mumbled softly. Atlas looked up, realising with regret that she was crying. Gods, he was such a cunt.

"I'm sorry. I'm so, so sorry, Eulalie. This is all my fault."

The woman curled up into him, making herself into a small ball on the bed. Atlas wrapped himself around her, feeling the strangeness of the sudden warmth that he knew he didn't deserve. He stroked her hair gently, moving his thumb back and forth over her head, and playing with her curls. Why did she want him to hold her? After all he did, Eulalie forgave him, just like that?

"I'm sorry," Atlas repeated. Like a broken fucking record. "I'm sorry. How can I make it up to you?" he asked, whilst Eulalie got up to face him.

"Let me do whatever I want to you for thirty seconds." she answered, almost immediately.

Atlas' eyes widened in fear.

What could she possibly want to do? *Why did she answer so fast?* What was she planning..? How selfish was it that he felt so unsafe with her, even though it was him that was the plain old abuser, the one that caused all this mess?

He shook away his panic, and nodded in agreement.

Lee smiled gratefully at him, wiping away her tears. She crouched opposite the boy, and held herself steady. In an instant, the woman smashed her fist into Atlas' face.

"*Fuck!* What the fuck are you doing?!" Atlas cried out, holding onto his nose, which was definitely bleeding. Eulalie ignored him, and swept out another punch.

Eulalie charged at him suddenly, an unknown beast attacking into him, striking him with her fist for ages. The weight of her hits forced the boy backwards, which only angered Lee more. She swung at his stomach, beating him senseless for what seemed like hours. Eulalie held him down with so much pressure the boy had to gasp for air; it kept going. And going. And going. Atlas counted in his head, loudly. The louder he counted, the less it ached. The more he counted, the sooner it would be all over. Atlas bit his lip, drawing more familiar red liquid, urging himself not to scream in pain. His brain told him it would only encourage her.

"Stop-! *Stop*!" he shouted out eventually, grabbing Lee's arms. "Please! It's been thirty-six seconds." he begged.

Atlas took a deep, well-needed breath, whilst the woman cracked her knuckles. His nose felt broken, and was bleeding onto Lee's bedsheets. He was sore everywhere - the boy's spine was screaming in pain from how he was positioned; doubled over, begging for mercy.

He looked up to Lee's face - so loving, and concerned for him.

"You're okay now, Atlas. You're okay." she muttered softly, caressing his cheek.

"But why...? Please... *why*?!" he said, holding onto her hand.

"Now we're even, you see?"

Atlas bit at his nails, and nodded. *Now we're even. We're okay. I'm okay.*

The boy didn't sleep as well that night. Soon after, the woman got changed and climbed into bed with Atlas. Eulalie insisted on cuddling in with him, holding him tightly as she drifted off to sleep. Everything fucking hurts.

14 -

The boy woke up to the sun shining through Lee's shitty curtains. He was alone in her bed, the cover all to himself, yet he never felt colder. Where was she?

Atlas sat up, but a pain stabbed into his head as he remembered last night. He sighed, staring at his body from underneath his shirt. He was bruised all over, his skin was black and purple in circle splodges. He looked disgusting. The boy shook his head - it was behind them, now. It was all okay. They were equal, now, like Eulalie said. They were all okay. He was *okay.*

The boy climbed out of bed and into the kitchen, where he saw Eulalie pouring over a letter, her back completely bent in, and her eyebrows furrowed. He sat up by the counter with her, muttering a 'good morning'.

"Morning, sleepyhead!" she smiled, rubbing his arm. "You slept in a while. It's eleven, like, fucking hell!" He smiled back weakly. He wasn't in the mood for her mindless conversation. Atlas looked down at her arms, glad to see that she had the sense to change over her bandages in the morning. One less thing he would have to deal with today.

He peered down at the letter Lee was reading. Everything was still blurry, but he could make out the first sentence; '..overdue on your water payment..' Lee rolled her eyes.

"You use way too much water. How am I going to pay this?" Eulalie shook her head in disbelief.

"Sorry," Atlas muttered.

"It's fine, you just need to pay me this month."

How was he meant to do that? He had fucked up the job interview, and Eulalie hadn't set him up with another. It didn't feel fair to blame it on her though - he was fully able to wander down to the dodgy off-licence shops himself and beg for a job.

"Atlas," she turned to face him.

The boy refused to meet her stare. "How am I meant to pay you?"

"I have ideas, don't worry."

Atlas looked up at her with a questioning look.

"First," she said, confidently, "first, I want you to tell me how the fuck you ended up here."

How he ended up here? Well.. that was a big question. He had to tell her eventually. It only felt right, as she was his best friend, his protector. And if this could count towards his payment to her.. that would be perfect.

"Well.. I reckon it started when my.. um, someone I knew got very, very ill." Atlas started. He didn't want to mention his sunflower just yet. She was too precious and.. it didn't feel right sharing her with Lee just yet. Lenore was all his.

"I started losing all hope, I guess. She was getting worse every week and I was just there. Watching her from across the room, watching her just loose more and more control of herself. The more medication and drugs the doctors gave her, the less she was actually alive, you know?

"So I met some weird people outside of school. They were like three or four years older than me and were all college drop-outs. They helped me cope.. but, maybe it wasn't in the best ways. Ada always supplied the group with vapes, then eventually when the head-high didn't hit anymore, we all moved onto cigs. I don't think I ever saw Albert and James sober. Victor was quiet and always sad, and we all knew it wasn't his real name.. but we liked him a lot. William, Kate, and Isabel were all skaters. Only thing I remember about Kate is that she got in trouble with the community police for graffitiing the skate park.

"Jupiter was my favourite. They came out as non-binary just before I joined the group and he, no, uh, *they* were still getting abuse for it. I'd like to think

I was the reason the abuse stopped. Got the shit beaten out of me for it, though. But I reckon, by doing that, I earnt everyone's respect. Everyone had that one person in the group they hung out with the most, the person they'd sit next to at the campfire. Jupiter was my person."

Eulalie scoffed at the name, but Atlas carried on.

"Then it all kind of went to shit when Victor brought in Robert, his boyfriend. He was a cutter and a burner, and he always walked around with his sleeves rolled high up. He even did it in front of us when he had a shit day. Rob was *royally* fucked up; so was everyone.. so.. our group turned a lot more depressive. Our hangouts turned into some scary thing where everyone brought their own.. well, you know, sharp things and we.. uh..."

Lee placed her hand on Atlas' arm, rubbing it in comfort. She urged him to go on.

"We'd sit underneath the outside train station stairs and cut ourselves as a group. It was fucking stupid. It turned into a fucking game. Victor always won. I can still remember it like yesterday.. It was disgusting but.. comfy.

"Jupiter never did it. They left when Robert started burning himself during our hangouts. It started so innocent - like a joke, like.. it started him just placing the burnt cig into his arm, or running past the flames we made with deodorant cans. But then he would get his lighter and just .. glide it across his arm like it was a normal thing that everyone did, like a fun game or something. But, yeah, Jupiter left and never came back. I wish I did that too. I wish I never joined the stupid games.

"Victor and Robert broke up soon after he was introduced to the group. They were never going to last - they were just each other's use of pleasure.

There was no real love in between them. Victor was the one that broke up the 'romance'.

"And then Robert killed himself two days later because of it. He did it under the outside train station stairs. He left a note in blood too, apparently. I can still remember the look on his face. He was smiling, white as a ghost, with sick poured down his face. He was completely naked, coated in thick, cold blood from his arms to his chest to his legs, His entire body was deflated and disgusting... every time I close my eyes I see his dead eyes staring back at me.

"William threw up at the sight of him. Victor only turned a very pale white, then walked out of the station. We never saw him again.

"We all knew Robert wanted us to see him die. He could have gone anywhere, but he chose the train station stairs. I don't think I've ever been the same since I saw his cold lifeless body leaning pathetically on the chained fence.

"Nobody left the group after that, though. It was like an addiction. Every Wednesday, Thursday, and Friday at four. I don't even remember what I was doing in my life at that point, I was like a fucking zombie. I thought it helped me cope, but I was just sinking further into the state Rob put himself into. It was only three days a week, and it was the highlight. For all the rest of the week, I would talk about it, research about it, watch videos, look at photos; it was all I could think about. But it got frustratingly boring when we all were running out of room.

"One day I went too far. Leno- um, the sick person got worse and the doctors were starting to send her back home to 'spend her moments with her family'. We all knew what that meant. I felt so shit, however instead of spending time with her, I hurt myself even more. I could have fucking died. I carved my arms and legs and my stomach. Just like Robert. I still have the scars - they're all lumpy and spread out far now. I look like a fucking freak. The group declared me the winner of the game.

"I gradually stopped going to school to see my friends more. Jupiter refused to talk to us and had broken all contact, Alexander and Madeline joined a bit later on - they always gave me nice things to drink, and the rest of us were all cut up and broken. My parents never saw my scars. I wore hoodies and baggy trousers.

"It was easy to hide away from my parents - they were barely at home. They took my.. friend on holiday all the time, all the places they wanted to go. And when they were home, they were far too occupied with her. I spent a lot of time alone in the house. My younger brother stayed with the neighbours next door, and I learned how to cook pot noodles when I was actually dying of hunger.

"But it all went to shit again when my parents received an attendance report from school. They had no idea I had completely dropped school - fucking off to random cities during the day instead with my mates. My Dad came home from all the nice sunny places, back into boring, rainy England to drive me to school everyday. I admit I felt kind of bad for that - but he still facetimed Mum all the time and I was pushed into the background yet again.

"During all of this, I felt like absolute shit. Everyone around me was about one blood drop away from dying or in total ignorance of my existence. I never ate anything and all I felt was misery eating at me day by day. Death was just around the corner for us all, and I was ready to accept it with open arms.

"School was shit, too. I made no friends and didn't go to a single class. Instead, I stayed with the IT guy called Richard and talked to him all day. We built a computer together; probably my greatest achievement. I genuinely got attached to him like crazy. He was my best friend and I felt like he was more than just a teacher. I told him so much, like what was going on with the sick person, my mental health.. but.. that's when I told him about the group and Robert.

"Police were called, social services, my parents, teachers, everyone. Everyone knew. My best friend had told safeguarding because of what I said to him.. what I showed him. I guess I'm the idiot for telling him. It's my fault.

"That day, when he told me he'd have to report it, I smashed up his IT room with a rounders bat I got from the PE department, before getting tackled down by security and excluded. I never saw Richard again.

"My parents dragged me home and cut off my clothes when I refused to take them off myself, and took photos of all my scars whilst I was naked. I shouted and they cried. They shouted and I cried. I tried running, but my Dad locked the bathroom door, and held me down. He changed all the locks and keys. The sick person was coming home that week, so they decided it would be easiest to send me to an inpatient for struggling teenagers. It probably would have helped if I let it. All I could think about was the next time I could hurt myself, it seemed like everyone else had that thought too.

"After four or five months, I finally got out after the hospital got shut down for not having enough funding, which kind of made sense. All the workers there acted like they were in a prison rather then just with normal humans that were struggling - they were underpaid to shit and didn't give a fuck. One group session they gave us all a sponge. A *fucking* sponge. To '*suck it up*'.

"The first week back, I couldn't stop cutting. I felt finally free to do what I wanted, finally free to cope.

My parents assumed I was fine now, after all those weeks at an inpatient; I was far from it. On a random afternoon, I was left alone to take care of my sick friend. So I slit my face open. I kept cutting and cutting until you could see parts of my teeth through the wound"

Atlas started to cry suddenly, tears dropping down his face uncontrollably. Through tears, he cried out;

"She fucking choked to death on vomit. She died and I could have saved her. You know what I was doing in the room next to her? Fucking cutting myself! *I could have saved her!*"

Atlas smashed his head onto the countertop. The memories all came flooding back to him. The way she tried to call out for help, the sound of her crashing down onto the floor. How she looked when she was seizing - twisting, shaking, pulling. The way she looked when she was dead. Cold. Peaceful. His shining sunflower, drooping at the petals, lifeless at the stem.

Eulalie patted his back like a Mother would, speaking soft comforts to him.

"After that.. I vowed to end it all. I removed all proof of my life, chucking my phone down a drain, tearing up all photos or evidence of the group and Jupiter. I escaped through the bathroom window on the first floor, and made my plan. My plan to kill myself.

"I was so close to doing it, so many times. But I failed. And now, now I'm here for some fucking reason," he sniffed.

Atlas took a deep breath.

He looked up at Lee, wanting more of her comfort and sweet words.

Silence. And then;

Eulalie huffed, saying; "You know, I think I miss when you never talked."

Atlas stared at her, trapped for words. He opened his mouth, then closed it again. The woman laughed at him, and returned to her letter. The boy sat, dead quiet, trying to supress his loud breathing as much as he could. Whatever made her happiest.

Just two weeks ago she told him how much she loved hearing him, though. How it made her feel like he was comfortable. Or did that even happen? Was it just wishful thinking, and he has actually been annoying her all the time? That seemed very likely.

"My God! And I thought I was the talkative one." she tutted, turning back to the bills. "I was expecting a one sentence answer. Oh my god.." Eulalie rolled her eyes and smiled.

15 -

Eulalie started doing sums on her phone, calculating up her bills. It didn't seem like a lot, but the boy had no idea of how much she made.

"You know, in the hour of you telling your nice little story, I could have made, like, a tenner."

"Sorry." Atlas responded, by default.

"Don't apologise. It doesn't do anything."

They sat in unnerving silence as Eulalie tapped at buttons on her phone. The numbers just kept getting bigger and bigger until they reached three digits. Atlas felt the guilt tugging at his chest - this could have been halved if it wasn't for him. What if, because of him, Eulalie was chucked out onto the streets?

Eulalie scoffed at him. "Stop looking so miserable, or I might have to start feeling bad for you. Anyway, that stuff, you said, are you lying to me?" Atlas shook his head. "So, if I were to call your parents, what would happen?"

"Don't."

The woman smiled down at her papers. "That's not the question. What would happen?"

"They'd isolate me. I'd never be allowed outside again. Or they'd send me somewhere." Atlas shivered in discomfort. He hated the way his friend gleamed when he told her such unnerving things. Maybe she just didn't care for him anymore. Maybe he had gotten boring. Or too outspoken.

Lee made a small noise of acknowledgment, before tutting at the papers again.

"Yeah, no, you're definitely going to have to help pay for this."

"I have forty quid in my bag," Atlas offered, but she just rolled her eyes at him again.

"I obviously already took that. Where else would all those bottles come from, dummy?"

"Oh," he muttered.

Eulalie snapped the notepads around her shut at once, and placed her phone back in her pocket. She went over to the coat hangers, and grabbed a woolly jacket.

Lee took a small hat, then opened the door. She looked behind her, inviting the boy to join her.

"I'm sick of all these stupid numbers. I want to go to the beach. Come with me?"

He put on a similar looking coat, running out the door with the woman. Sometimes it was nice to be alone - but this wasn't the time. He could feel all the thoughts getting ready to stab into him as soon as his protector, his friend left the apartment. Atlas wasn't ready for it. He stepped out of the dark house, feeling its clouds of regret and anxiety wafting further and further away from him.

It had been a while since he had gone outside. The last time was for the job interview and that was barely a walk. So many days and weeks had passed Atlas had no idea what happened when, it was all just an uncoordinated blur, trudging in the background.

Lee guided the two of them to the beach, where it was grey and windy. The sky was slowly seeping into a casual winter day, clouds hovering over what could have been a beautiful blue sky. It was freezing, the cold biting at Atlas' body - sending goose bumps down his neck. The fresh air felt salty and reviving - something the boy never thought he'd ever appreciate, and the sound of crashing waves brought him back down, so that he was present, he was here, in the moment; it was okay. Everything was okay.

They took deep breaths together as they sat against rocks. In, and out. Atlas watched dogs trot around happily, awaiting commands from their masters who followed behind shortly. In, and out. Lee pointed out two people surfing into the high waves, laughing as one of them smacked right off the board and into the icy cold water. In, and out. The boy closed his eyes, shutting off his brain completely.

Here, by the sea, everything was fine. Him and Lee weren't fighting here. No arguments, no stupid snidely comments. Just peaceful nothingness. He knew Eulalie was thinking the same thing exactly, because she was refusing to say a single word to him - worried that it would start something.

Atlas snapped out of his brain when Eulalie jumped up from the rocks. The boy watched as she walked over to a man who looked around her age, and pulled him in for a hug.

"Arch, no, Atlas, come meet Roderick!" she beckoned him over, and chatted happily to the man.

He greeted the man with an awkward smile, being introduced as the 'roommate with benefits' by Eulalie. He wasn't sure what that meant.

Roderick towered over Eulalie with his height, but to Atlas he was only a bit tall. He had bluey-purple dyed hair with brown roots growing at the top. His beard was bushy and unkept; growing in uneven patches towards the front. He wore a cropped black leather jacket that had pins and patches all of different bands; *P!NK*, *Green Day, Blink 182*, and *Sparky Deathcap*.

If Atlas were to guess, he was probably in his late twenties. His face was beginning to show signs of wrinkles and stress, but the way he stood, the way he presented himself made him seem a lot younger. He supposed the same could be said for Eulalie.

"You must be the Archie I've been hearing so much of!" he smiled, then correcting himself to 'Atlas' instead. Roderick spoke in a heavy northern accent; at times it was difficult to understand what he was asking of Atlas. "My God, you really are a handful aren't you? Eulalie tells me so much about you." He then turned to the woman and said quietly with a smirk; "Little young for *you* I would have thought?"

The boy looked uneasily at Lee; she only laughed at him.

"Stop looking so miserable, I said. Let's walk down the shore."

As they walked, Atlas found out from the two friend's conversation that Roderick was a 'soon to be successful' drummer from the local bars. He had been planning with his friends for about five years now to make it big in Brighton, and it kind of felt like the only thing he would ever talk about. Whilst waiting for the hits to get the recognition they deserved, he said, he was working at an Infant School nearby as a cleaner.

Eulalie listened to him patiently without pausing, letting him rant about all the problems that were happening in the band: how they didn't have a singer anymore, how the bassist was a total dick, and how nobody even cared as much as Roderick did. Atlas wondered how he hadn't given up on his dreams yet, and a small look from Eulalie told him that she thought the exact same thing.

They walked all the way back to the apartment, all together. Roderick was fine. He was nice enough, he just never said anything else except for the band. He was just a bit tiring.

"Woah, I haven't been here in ages. I remember I showed you my first song right here, remember? 'The Gold-Bug'?" Roderick exclaimed, stepping into the living room. The boy saw his face fall just a millimetre when he realised Eulalie had disappeared into the bathroom.

Roderick sat himself on the sofa, admiring the apartment by himself.

"So..." the man said, after a pause. "So... how long have you guys been.. you know."

"What do you mean?" Atlas joined him on the sofa.

"You know what I mean. Going out. Seeing each other." he nudged the boy playfully.

"What? We don't 'go out'?!" Atlas said, a little too fast.

Roderick chuckled, muttering 'sure, sure' under his breath. He grinned at Atlas and winked.

"Genuinely. We don't- I don't like dating."

"Well.." he said, slowly. "I'm just going off of what Eulalie has said to me."

Atlas' ears pricked up in surprise. What had she been saying to him? To all her friends? That they were going out? It couldn't be further from the truth. They were just friends. He knew he didn't like anyone in that way, especially Lee. She was a Mother to him, for Gods' sake!

Just then, Eulalie came out of the bathroom and started boiling some water. Atlas made a mental note to definitely bring that up with her later. She brought over two coffees for herself and Roderick, and a sickly sweet hot chocolate for Atlas which he refused to even try.

"Getting along?" Lee smirked, recognising the discomfort in Atlas' eyes.

"I think somebody's in denial." Roderick said, in a sing-song voice that irritated the boy. Atlas shook his head, scowling at the man. "Yes you are! You made her a cake on her birthday with 'I love you' written on it, and don't even get me started on the gifts. You are such a sweetheart."

"What?!" Atlas turned to face Lee quickly. "What have you told him? You know I didn't do that."

Eulalie elbowed Roderick in the ribs, glaring at him threateningly. He looked back at her, confused and annoyed. He picked up his back, and checked his watch.

"Okay, well.." he scratched his head awkwardly. "Oh, is that the time? I better be off. Don't get me involved in this, Lee. I promise you I don't care," and walked to the door. Roderick laughed softly to himself, and strode out the door - leaving Atlas eyeing the woman angrily.

"What the fuck did you tell him?" he demanded as soon as the door slammed shut.

Eulalie seemed furious at the sudden outburst from the boy. "I didn't tell him anything!" she screamed back, scrambling for words.

Atlas jumped up from the sofa, covering his eyes with his hands. "Why the fuck are you going around your friends, telling them we're dating?!"

The woman got up too, and grabbed Atlas' arms. "Maybe I just wanted some excitement?! Maybe I wanted my friends to think I wasn't fucking lonely?!" She dug her nails into his skin; it took a lot of control not to cry out for her to stop. She was not winning this time, Atlas urged himself.

He pulled away anyway, stepping back from her. "Get away. Stop talking to your friends about me! And if you can't stop lying about me, then maybe you shouldn't be seeing them!" he yelled. Atlas backed up away from her, ending up at the wall whilst Lee moved closer to him.

"What, am I not allowed to have friends anymore? Should I just phone your parents and you can go back with them?! Is that what you want?

Atlas paused.

"Tell me!" she screamed. "Cause if it is, I'll phone them up, right now."

The boy stared down at the floor, feeling anxiety building up inside him. He merely shook his head, earning a vicious laugh from the woman. He saw, from the corner of his eye, Eulalie reaching in from her pocket and dialling a number. He saw, from the corner of his eye, Lee pointing the phone to his face and hovering her finger over the call button.

The boy's heart starting beating twice as fast. The number was his Mother's. She was really going to do this, wasn't she?

"No.. no, please. Don't do that. You have no idea." he begged, crumpling down to the floor.

"God, I have you completely trapped, don't I?" Lee giggled. She rested her hand on the wall where Atlas kneeled, paralysed in worry. "Atlas." she whispered. "Atlas!" Lee repeated. The boy looked up at her. The woman saw the fear pulsing throughout his body, shimmering around his eyes.

Eulalie backed away from him, and rolled her eyes. "You really think that low of me?" She turned off the phone and shoved it back in her pocket. "I would never do that to you." She collapsed backwards onto the sofa, huffing and muttering to herself.

The boy stayed knelt down at the wall, until Lee commanded him away from it. She picked out a movie for them to watch, 'Legally Blonde', and Atlas fell asleep with his head rested on her shoulder. Atlas felt the hatred pulsing through his body, mixing deeply with the guilt he created himself. It was his fucking fault; did he really think that lowly of his friend? The one who had given him shelter and love?

He awoke only a few hours later to soft cries from Eulalie. Tears fell down from her puffy red eyes. She was holding onto the boy gently for support, burying her head into Atlas' neck. His guilt burnt stronger, sinking into his gut.

"Hey.." he said, lifting her head up. "What's going on?"

"I'm s-sorry.." Eulalie whimpered. "I just.. can't b-believe you'd think I'd do that to you." She stared up at him, waiting for him to say something. "Aren't you.. g-gonna say sorry to me?"

"I'm sorry." Atlas said without hesitation.

The boy held her even tighter as she cried into his arms. How the fuck did he end up here?

16 -

"I'm the worst person ever," Eulalie sobbed. It had taken the boy about two whole hours trying to calm her down, even offering himself as stress relief; he was glad that she denied that, as his older bruises still churned and ached against his clothes. But here she was again, a cut in Atlas' clothes had set her off, and she was in tears again.

The boy sighed to himself, knowing he shouldn't be so selfish. Eulalie had done so much for him, the least he could was support and love her, but he couldn't even do that. No, all he would do is make her angry. This was all his fucking fault.

"Atlas.." she wept, looking into his eyes. In her eyes, Atlas saw himself - a scarred, black and blue boy shivering in distress. He saw his own face - warped in the tears, disgusting and selfish. "Atlas," she repeated to herself, thinking deeply. "I guess that name suits you more.."

Eulalie crawled into his lap, placing her head into the boy's lap. She gazed up at him with a half-assed smile. Atlas didn't even deserve that.

"I'm sorry," she said.

"I'm sorry too."

"I think I have problems. It's not my fault, you know. It sucks being alone. That's why I told him about.. us." she paused, waiting for Atlas' reaction.

The boy hesitated, not wanting to make her even sadder: "There is no 'us'." he said, flatly.

"You think I don't know that? I know, okay?" Lee whispered furiously, tears choking her again. "And it makes me feel like shit. Nobody fucking loves me. I have, like, really bad abandonment trauma. It sucks having people who don't care about me."

"I care about you, I swear."

Eulalie huffed, and closed her eyes.

A minute of calming silence passed by with Eulalie in his lap, staring into the ceiling, when all of a sudden;

"I like you angry, by the way. You're hot."

He sat up, quickly. What did that even mean? Hot as in attractive? Hot as in... temperature? Hot as in, just not at all, and making fun of him? What the fuck did she mean by that? He shot her a grim look, head tilted to which she only laughed.

"What do you mean?"

"When. You're. Angry. You're. Hot." She spoke slowly, pronouncing each syllable carefully like he was deaf. It made him want to swing a punch into her patronising face.

Atlas pushed her off his lap in a way he hoped was not seen as playful. This was not the right time. Not at fucking all.

He winced as she sat up too, and leaned over towards him - rubbing his bruised arm hard.

"Stop," he rolled his eyes, trying to play it all off as a joke. "Stop!" he said again, with more urgency as Eulalie shuffled closer towards him on the sofa. "You're weird." he laughed anxiously. He could almost hear the shaking in his voice echoing around the room. He didn't want to laugh. He wanted to yell, tell her to *piss off*, tell her to leave him alone.

Eulalie pushed him up against the sofa arm, holding his legs down. She climbed into his lap again, but this time closer, and sat on his thighs.

"Lee-"

She cupped his face with her hands, scratching his face with her nails. Atlas fought to urge to flinch. The woman smirked at him, edging closer to him.

"Why are you- what are you doing? Why are you on me?" Atlas muttered with panic trembling in his voice. The so frequent fear built up in him again, prickling against his skin whenever she grazed against him. His breathe quickened, torso rising up and down with intensity. He was going to be sick. He was going to pass out, this was the end. He was going to die. Right here, right now.

"Just relax." Eulalie responded, shuffling closer and closer - like an animal hunting, like a monster creeping. Soon, their heads were only a few centimetres apart; Atlas could feel her breath on his lips.

A familiar chill ran down his spine. What is happening? What is she doing?

She started to hold his waist, squeezing, grabbing, gripping tight so he couldn't move. As she held against his thighs, suddenly, it felt like Eulalie's hands weren't hers anymore. They were the boys' from the alleyway. The way they held him down - the way they spoke to him, trying to do whatever they wanted to do. But that was different, right? The boys.. they were dangerous. Eulalie wouldn't hurt him, ever.

"Lee- please stop. I don't know what you're doing."

"It's okay, I was scared too, but it's okay." Eulalie kept repeating every time he raised his panicked voice.

"Wait, what do you mean?!" he yelled, shoving her away from him. She landed on the other side of the sofa, looking pleased with herself. Everything was starting to make sense.

"God, I love it when you bite back."

"For fuck's sake!" he shouted, staying frozen, terrified on the sofa. "Lee, I'm fifteen! Fucking fifteen! Are you trying to have *sex with me?!*"

Eulalie's face hardened, frowning angrily at him. Her face turned red, but she refused to loose eye contact. "You think I'm a weirdo or some shit? No! No, we're just having fun?! Everyone does this, you just have no *fucking* friends so *of course* you wouldn't know." she grumbled back, low in volume but even more petrifying.

"Plus," she carried on, "plus, you owe me. If you have fun with me, then that can count towards your payment for rent."

She paused for a second, watching Atlas with intent. "I'm being *really* fucking generous here."

"Lee, this is fucking *ridiculous*-"

"So you'd rather go back to your parents? Back to your little suicide group, and the hospital? 'Cause that's *completely fucking fine*. I have the number. Saved in my contacts actually. Just say the word, and I'll call them up! Or don't, be a bitch about it, and I'll call them anyway." she grimaced, reaching over to the coffee table to get her phone.

Atlas stood very still, solid as steel, as she picked up her phone and entered in the number.

Fuck.

"So, what should it be? Take my extremely generous offer, or go fuck off back to wherever shithole you came from? I don't mind either way, you don't affect me in the slightest. Maybe it would be nice not having you around, following my every step like a pathetic *dog*," she spat, narrowing her eyes at the boy.

Atlas shook his head, very slowly.

"Please don't call them. I'll take your offer."

As soon as he said this, Eulalie regained her happy demeanour, chucking her phone to the side and crawling back onto Atlas' lap.

"What are we going to do..?" he whispered.

Eulalie grinned at him, pushing against his thighs and touching his waist.

This was happening. This was happening now, and there was nothing he could do about it . This was happening, and he had to go along with it. This was happening - it had to happen, otherwise she would send him back. Lee was better than anything back at home. Lee was amazing. Lee was lovely, and his protector. She never meant any harm. Right?

He tried distancing himself from the world - trying to remember the effects of the drug he longed for. Atlas begged for the distance it gave him. The dream-like state he had to pull himself back from. But this wasn't a dream. This was a crippling sleep paralysis, holding him down forcefully and prodding against his ugly, twisted skin. No matter how many times he screamed at himself to run, or to fight her, he sat on the sofa, accepting what came to him.

Atlas felt tears dropping down his cheek as Lee lifted off his shirt. He felt the fabric brush against his scarred body, watching Eulalie's face fall at the sight of his disgusting body. She grimaced, stopping for only a second; muttering a small "Oh,", as Atlas rushed to pull down his shirt again despite her look of annoyance. Goosebumps rattled all the way across his body and a wave of anxiety shot through him every breath she took, every touch.

How the fuck did this happen? A hundred miles from home, sitting on a patched up, stained sofa, with what he thought was his protector, who was now trying to pull off his shirt. His guardian. A sister to him. A mother.

Eulalie looked at the boy's skeleton-like body with desire and hunger burning in her eyes. She traced every scar with her fingertips, scratching with her nails where it was just plain skin. Eulalie smiled to herself, having the small boy to herself.

"Atlas?"

He refused to meet her eyes.

"Have you ever kissed somebody before?"

He refused to answer her.

Lee forced his head up, gazing into the pleading brown eyes of the boy. She tugged at his neck, pulling him closer into her lips. He shook his head, attempting to tell her not to, when she closed her eyes and kissed him softly.

The woman played it safe - gently brushing against his lips. Maybe, in different circumstances, he'd actually be grateful for her. *What the fuck was wrong with him?* Eulalie was stunning. Any boy would have been so happy to have her kissing him. Lee was so kind to him, perfect, beautiful. Everything and anything he could have ever needed or wanted. So why did he feel so disgusted? Like she said... everyone does this. Right?

When she moved away from him, she looked up and down at the small boy. Half naked, bruised and cut up. Pale skin, matted hair and yellow teeth, dangerously bony; you could count every rib-cage. Trembling from head to toe, curled up as close as he could into a ball without Eulalie noticing.

The woman stood up from the sofa, and walked to her bedroom.

"You're kinda cute. I could get used to this." Eulalie smiled, slamming the door behind her.

The loud bang didn't even make him jump. He sat, unmoving, petrified, with tears scratching against his cheek; whilst his brain struggled anxiously to make any sense of what just happened. Atlas tried not to cringe - his best friend had just seen his body. Ugly, deformed, disgusting. She probably wouldn't want him in the house anymore. He just hoped to himself that she wouldn't want to see his body again.

The body clung on to his shirt as if it were going to fall off him. He stretched it down onto the sofa, puling it over his legs, curling himself into a small ball. The material comforted him against the phantom feelings of Eulalie's soft hands upsetting his skin.

He felt her touch still lingering, like a slow poison. It lurked eagerly, sending forces of shivers and vomit creeping around his body. He still felt her hands on him.

Atlas rushed to the bathroom, over to the sink, making sure to lock the door as he entered. The boy took off his shirt in a hurry, and placed his frail hands beneath the cold water. He tried not to make a single sound - what if she came back? Decided she wasn't done - decided that what he did wasn't enough for the rent?

He grabbed his wrist - kneading and pulling it; gently at first, but as he realised her touch wasn't fading away, the rubbing got harder and harder, until his wrist turned red raw. Atlas splashed the cold water onto his chest, but the cool liquid only seemed to make the feeling so much worse - not only was her touch still there, but he felt her squeezing, grabbing, pulling.

Atlas stripped off his trousers, too. He drenched himself in the water - now scratching at his legs. She was still there. On him. Her sickening hands were still playing with his thighs - fiddling with his blotched scars, persistently holding him down into the sofa.

How could he not remember every detail? Her face, pleased and proud with herself. Her words, dangerous but soft at the same time. His anxiety - so engulfing yet he did nothing to stop her. He sat and took it. It was all his fucking fault. It flooded his brain, drowning any other thought, thundering ugly visions; warped, untrue.

Though his skin was beginning to give way, the touch stayed still. Determined to ruin him. The boy dropped to the floor in an instant, the bathroom growing smaller and smaller. Her hands were still on him. He had to get them off his skin, still prickling in discomfort.

The room was only getting more cramped, like he was running out time. He had to do something. As if, if he didn't, the touch wold sink in, never ever leaving him. His heart beat fast - vibrating powerfully. His blood swam around his body. Begging to be released.

The moment he noticed the razor, a clear solution was found.

The boy's body shuddered in anticipation. Atlas grabbed the razor and played with it in his hand, feeling it glide in between his fingers like an old friend. The corners of his mind closed, easing him into the blade, guiding him into it. It had been far too long.

Atlas gasped as he made the first cut. He carved a small incision just above where Eulalie had held him down - gliding, sailing smoothly across his thigh. Small counts of blood dropped down his leg, creating a warm red puddle just to his right. Atlas moved down his thigh through the cut, going under it and peeling back his skin.

The sudden pain brought tears to his eyes once more - but he shook in excitement. He peeled back his skin like a sunburn - stopping for only a second at each pull. Each chunk of himself he pulled off felt like more freedom - Eulalie wasn't on him anymore, she was on the bloody bathroom floor. Atlas felt more free from her, the more he mutilated himself. It felt so worth it.

His brain stopped flashing back to the sofa; instead staying in the moment, enjoying every moment, every ounce of torture the boy was inflicting on himself. It was alluring to him.

His thighs were a raw bloody mess - blood bubbling and rolling off his legs. His thigh's epidermis was completely peeled back, leaving only crimson red patches in his skin.

The pain felt unbearable, uncontrollable, terrifying. But it was beautiful. It *was* controlled. This pain, he did it. He was in control of the pain. He was finally in control. He could only watch from a third person perspective as a small boy in a small bathroom bled out large amounts of beautiful blood. It wasn't real; so there were no consequences. It wasn't him.

The panic couldn't reach him. In this moment, and this one only, Atlas felt at ease. He watched the young boy curl up into a ball, admiring the work he had done.

Atlas cried into his bloody legs. This is where he belonged. He wanted to die, right there, now. What a perfect end that would be. It would release him of the woman who he thought was a friend. Atlas had wanted to die, so badly, for years now. Maybe now, maybe right now. This was the time. He was going to end it all.

The boy picked up the blood stained razor for his last time. This had to be the end - right? There was no other way he could realistically get away from his situation. Eulalie would do unimaginable things if she found Atlas still alive but in this condition. She would hate him, and he would have to watch her face crumple and cry as she found him drooping, near death, over a razor. If he were dead, he was gone. He wouldn't have to deal with her reaction. Maybe that was selfish. But maybe he just didn't care anymore.

Atlas pressed the razor into his thigh, testing the pain. The razor, sharper than a sword, ran through his body like butter - flawlessly slicing in a perfect straight line. He repeated the process, digging his nails into his arm when the cut stung out. He got braver with each cut, until he couldn't even see his leg anymore. Everywhere around him was coated in blood; yet it still wasn't enough. Not nearly enough.

If he just had the courage to cut up a vein, an artery. Then he could just *die* so much faster. But even the thought of touching such a sensitive part of himself with a blade threatened vomit. Instead, he struck further into his body elsewhere.

Atlas hacked at his thighs and waist, moving onto his arms when he felt as though he was finished. He grimaced and held back his breath as he slashed from his wrist to his forearm in one cut. The red liquid sprayed everywhere - bubbling onto his already stained clothes. The rest of his wounds dripped so gently, racing down his legs peacefully.

Her touch was so far away from him now. The boy had ripped it off with the small razor. Her touch was hacked off him - lying somewhere in the piles of blood and chunks of skin and flesh.

Atlas stared up at the ceiling. *Was it enough? Did he do enough?*

It didn't feel like dying. It all felt far too peaceful for death.

17 -

The boy slipped in and out of consciousness, making time move rapidly. Vision blurred, mind dreary, all he could see were blotches of red circling him, a pathetic puddle sitting under his thighs. Blood oozed out, fast at first; and then, slower, and slower. But he wasn't dead.

Atlas watched as it splattered onto the tiles - bit by bit, the stain growing larger every minute. Eulalie would kill him - how would she clean up all his mess? How selfish was he really - leaving her to deal with all this mess? But he wasn't dead. He wasn't leaving her.

Drip, drip, drip.

Hours passed. Hours that felt like only seconds, but the room around him wasn't blurring out, not fading. He felt more alive than ever - his thighs burning like a wild fire. He was like an arsonist; caught in his own destruction. The bathroom was as bright as ever - he could see everything, so clearly.

No, he wasn't dead. Not in the slightest. He had failed. Again.

Knock, knock, knock.

"Archie? No, fuck, Atlas?" a small voice came calling.

Shit.

"I'm coming in."

She walked in, slowly at first, and then, as soon as she saw the red splattered everywhere - the woman sped over to the boy. Eulalie looked at him, up and down, but her face showed no emotion. It was blank, eerily empty. What was she thinking? Was she disappointed? Scared? Angry? Atlas didn't even feel the embarrassment wash through him when Lee's eyes lingered for a second too long on his uncovered body. It didn't feel like his own body anymore - he was so embedded with blood and cuts that there was barely a body there at all.

For the first time in a while, Lee had no words. She spoke no cruel remarks, no snide comments. It made Atlas feel a sudden shot of pride - just for a second - when he understood that Eulalie was finally out of her depths, before burying that gross feeling deep inside him.

I'm dangerous, I'm unpredictable. You can't save me. I do it so much better than you do. Look at my wounds, and want them. You don't know how to help me. I'm worse than you, more ill. I win. He didn't dare say a word, scared a thought might slip out his mouth.

After a while, she sighed and she sat him up on the bath ledge, examining the cuts. From the medicine cabinet above the toilet, she pulled out a huge roll of bandages, and then a bottle of antiseptic. She knelt down, in front of him, and silently worked her way up; gently applying a stinging amount of gel onto the cuts, then covering them with the bandages.

The two said nothing at all - but that was enough for them both. Atlas saw a flicker of panic and anger flash through her eyes, her face falling for just a split second. He should have felt guilty. But he felt nothing, except the stabbing pain of all his wounds being strangled into him with the bandages. It was comforting.

"I can't trust you anywhere except here right now. I know you'll just cut yourself the second I leave for work, so you'll have to stay here." Eulalie said confidently, avoiding his eyes when she had placed on the last bandage. Atlas gave no response.

"I know this is hard for you, but it'll be okay." The woman left the bathroom, taking with her the razors, scrubs, and flower pots. He heard the rustling of furniture the second she exited, and then, finally, the slam of the front door.

The room was exactly the same. Nothing had changed, the blood was still swimming in itself on the bathroom tiles, the walls and mat stained a sickly crimson. Nothing was different, except a substantially less amount of sharp things, and about a hundred more used bandages placed on the boy.

Atlas had failed. *Again*. Did he even go that deep? Eulalie refused to let him look at the cuts - slapping his hand away when he tried to poke at them. Something went wrong. He didn't do it right.

Why wasn't he sad? Why didn't he try again? His mind urged him to find something else. Anything else. Even the bathtub could have been enough - even the sink. If he could just crack his head open on the ledges - fucking *hang himself* with his towel.

His body stayed perfectly still; eyes forward, legs unshaking. He should have died. He should have died this night, but he should have been gone long before. On that fucking bridge. That stupid old man.

Why did he listen to him? Why did he stop? What the fuck was wrong with him - did he do it for attention all along? Do enough damage to freak someone out - stay alive for just long enough to make them feel even worse?

He sat, unmoving. Colour faded from his body - leaving pale, warped skin, and disgusting, mutilated cuts.

His brain was dead - that was for certain. Atlas had no thoughts rushing through his brain any longer; only fuzzing ambience whirring in between his ears like dust collecting. Whispers of threats - murmurs and mutterings of urges.

The stinging never left him, pricking his skin and rustling against the bandages. The pain was the only thing grounding him, it seemed. Maybe, in a way, the pain was keeping him alive. Alive and human. Because this was how he coped - as fucked up as it was. This was how he coped. And it wasn't anything more than that - he couldn't end his life like this. This was how he kept himself alive.

Atlas thought back to what the two of them did, last night. Whatever happened next, he knew, he'd have to deal with it. Whatever Eulalie wanted to do to him; he deserved it. He deserved it, and far worse. He would have to sit tight and deal with her touch - her lips against his. Maybe he didn't even mind it - he was just being dramatic, perhaps it was just the boys in the alley he was so terrified of. Maybe he actually liked it - his brain was attention seeking, reminding the boy of the nightmarish ways the boys held down his thighs forcefully - trying to take off his clothes.

No. No, Lee wasn't like that. What happened last night... it was consensual, right? Atlas didn't really say no, and if he did, he obviously didn't make it clear enough to her. She just didn't know he was uncomfy. It was his fault all along. As usual.

It would take time, and effort. But he could do that, for her. This could be his payment to her, his protector, for forcing her to see the disgusting mutilation he did to himself.

Atlas felt his eyes drooping. He fell asleep - skin grazing against the bandages that made him look like a mummy, alone and cold in a bathtub.

He didn't know how long he slept for, but it didn't matter. Because when he awoke, Eulalie was gone.

When he woke up, he waited for her to barge into the bathroom and interrupt his peace; planning to himself on how he would react to her presence. But after hours of waiting, he finally decided to get out of the cold bathtub and make himself known, as Eulalie was not coming to him. The boy limped over to the bathroom door, and pulled down on the handle hard. It took all his strength to weigh down the old handle, his body weight melting into the floor as he pulled. But it didn't even matter - when he pushed to leave the room, Atlas felt a heavy object leaning into the door, a sofa or something blocking the door from moving. She had blocked him in. Like a fucking animal, like a dog.

The worst part was, he knew he could have moved the furniture out of the way. But his bones were weary - he was exhausted, hurting, starving. So he slid back into the bathtub, pathetically, and waited for his protector to come back to him. Even after a long night out; she always came back - even if it meant she was high, or drunk, or bleeding. She always came back.

And she did, but... not to him. After a while, maybe a day, she came back into the apartment. He kept hearing her throughout the week, slamming the door as she entered and exited, singing her stupid songs as she went about her day, cooking powerful-smelling meals, getting on with her life as if there wasn't a half-dead teenage boy locked in her bathroom. Her songs burnt into the boy's ears - letting her voice play on and on and on in his mind for hours on end. Everything Atlas heard her do, say, sing; it felt calculated, as if she was taunting him. But he didn't say a word.

All he could really do on his own was sleep and think. He had a lot to think, a whole ton to remember and cringe at, too many memories to be miserable at, but he was too tired to cry anymore. Atlas didn't bother wasting his fumbling energy on the door again - the boy knew he was too weak to even move it an inch. So instead... three steps to the door, one to the window and then a pull up. Fifteen floor tiles, all equally smothered in blood. Three-hundred and seventy four leaves, from the wall vines to the small potted plants that were quickly removed. Six hundred and something bricks. Forty-nine bandages, wrapped around his decrepit body. Holding his body together.

When she came back from wherever she went, obviously drunk, Lee still used the bathroom, obviously. The night she got back, woman pulled back the sofa that was keeping the boy in, and refused to acknowledge him. She acted as though he was never there.

But he was! He was there, he wanted to cry out to her. His heart would flutter and beat twice as fast whenever he saw the handle lower - though he never dared show it. He just wanted a bit of attention from her, a smile, a nod in his direction, anything! He stayed put, lying still, unmoving, barely letting himself breathe let alone talk.

The only thing Lee did to recognise the boy's existence was slip him a meal, twice a day, without looking at him at all.

Days like this passed, painfully slow. Every time Eulalie went into the bathroom, it was the highlight of his day. Not seeing anyone, let alone anything except the blood-stained freezing bathroom, he had grown obsessive over Lee. She was his protector, after all. The only one who could get him out of this mess. He'd even started to starve himself, just so his protector would stay with him just a bit longer to make sure he actually ate the food until she realised this trick, and refused to stay with him any longer than just placing down the dish, and leaving at once.

Whenever the woman entered the miserable room, he wanted to scream, shout, beg for forgiveness, to ask what he did wrong, what he could possibly ever do for her to forgive him. But he said nothing.

This was how Lee was making him pay. Days went by, he was all alone. No words, no touch, not even eye contact. Nothing.

But isn't this what he wanted? For her to leave him alone, to stop being all 'weird'? No, this isn't what he wanted. Hours trudged by and boredom lunged at him - with nothing to do, all he could do was think. He thought about how lonely he was, he thought about all the memories that haunted him, he thought about how ungrateful he was, and how much he wanted Lee to look at him again, for one fucking second, he would do anything, just for that.

Was this on purpose? Or did she really not know what to do with him anymore?

He just wanted Lee again. Atlas even started wishing for her to be weird with him again. Anything that made her happy. Anything to make Atlas feel a little bit more wanted. He'd do anything for her, if she just...

please, for fuck's sake, just look at me. I'm right here. Look at me. I'm real. I'm here. And I would do everything, and anything, if you just smiled at me.

Three steps to the door, but it was properly around thirty now; he hadn't walked in days and his feet felt glued to the bath. Fifteen floor-tiles, all equally smothered in blood. Five steps to the window, although even the thought of pulling himself up tired him out. Forty-eight bandages - one had peeled off. Six-hundred and eighty nine bricks.

Eventually, it all got too much. Her quick appearances and disappearances drove him mad. The singing and all her signs of life drove him mental. But here he was, locked in the room, all alone. So, after a week of nothingness, just misery melting into the disgusting bathtub he never strayed from, all his words came tumbling out all at once.

Atlas climbed out of the bathtub when he saw the sun hit a certain angle, and smelt the wafts of food being cooked, sitting down by the door like a dog waiting for its owner. This was his specific routine, to show he still cared. He still liked her. He wanted her. She was his protector, maybe not like a mother anymore.. she had ruined that.

Atlas' ears pricked up at once as he heard small footsteps making their way over to the bathroom door. The boy felt his excitement rapidly increasing, his heart shuddering and face gleaming with excitement. Lee was coming. His favourite person, his best friend.

The door opened slowly, she walked into the room and carelessly flopped down a plastic plate full of pasta and sauce. Eulalie began to turn and leave, not giving him a single glance, when all of a sudden, fear shot through Atlas' body - prickling up his spine and sending goose bumps rattling against the tightly wrapped bandages. If he didn't act quick, she would leave for the night, and wouldn't be back for hours. He knew her routine; he had memorised it. If he didn't act quick, he would be so isolated, and he was so restless for Eulalie's attention.

In a hurry, he grabbed Lee's ankle, forcing her to look down at the boy, who was wrapping himself into her leg and starting to sob. She looked down at the boy, all bandaged up and bloodied due to the cuts leaking out, and the bandages hadn't been changed. His body was somehow even skinnier than before, resembling almost perfectly a skeleton. His arms and legs were so disgustingly bony and tiny that they looked like you could just snap them in half easily.

"Please," the boy begged, sobbing noisily, but refusing to break eye contact with the woman, like he would never look at her again. "*Love me again.* I don't know what I did wrong," Atlas wailed. "I am sorry. *Please, please.. please*," the boy cried out.

Atlas' heart practically stopped when he saw her kneel down to where the boy sat, and although she shook him off and pushed him away, she held his hands, stroking them with her thumbs, comforting him. She ran her fingers through his matted, greasy hair, and sat him back down on the tiled floor.

"Atlas." She spoke softly, yet annoyance was nagging at the back of her throat. "Atlas, why are you acting like this? I thought you hated me."

He shook his head at once: "What?! Hate you?! No, no.. no I don't. I definitely don't. You *locked* me in here and I-"

"I locked you in here for a day, when I went to work, like I said," Eulalie told him, calmly. "I got rid of the sofa as soon as I got back. You could've just.. left it. Why didn't you just try again later? I just assumed you hated me and were refusing to leave the bathroom..."

"No..! No- I didn't.. I didn't know!" His words fumbled together, voice straining and breaking already. It had been days since he had spoken a word. "I'm sorry. I'm so, so sorry. I didn't know."

Eulalie leaned back against the wall, shaking her head in disbelief. She ran her hand through her hair and closed her eyes. "I don't think sorry is enough," Lee sniffed. "You did this to yourself - to what.. to guilt trip me? Atlas..."

He crawled over to her right away. The boy wanted to hold onto to her and never let go. "I know it's not enough. I'm not enough. I'm sorry. I should have tried the door again."

"And what about this?!" The blue-haired woman gestured to the mess of the bathroom, eyes widening. "You're doing this on purpose to hurt me. I can't stand it. You know my weaknesses and use them against me, Atlas. You are evil!" Lee started to stand up, but the boy reached out to her hand, hanging limply by her side.

"Please don't leave me here. I'm sorry. I'll better myself. I'll be better for you."

She only sighed, retracting her hand from the boy. But as she gazed down at him, the sickly, greasy-haired, bloodied boy, pity sank into her chest. She helped him up cautiously, catching him when he tumbled, and walked him on out of the bathroom, and into her bedroom.

The apartment had never looked better. Everything was more colourful, more attractive. Winter sunshine shone through the windows, which were decorated head to toe in papers coloured with trees and presents and candy canes. The sunset gleamed pinks and golds, flooding the living room with such warmth and beauty - such perfection Atlas had never seen before, never appreciated. He could hear, clearer now, the belts of ABBA playing in the background. It reminded him of his first days here. Everywhere was warm, welcoming, loving. He would never disregard the beauty of the apartment, ever again. He would never step foot in that horrible bathroom, ever again.

How could he be so stupid, anyway? Did he really think Lee would do such a cruel thing to him, after all of the angelic things she had done for him; take him in, feed him, give him water and a bed, all for a small price of having fun with her? How could he be so fucking ungrateful, and try to end his life.. just because his friend wanted payment for rent? Maybe he didn't even deserve to be out of that room... Lee was so generous, so kind.

Eulalie rummaged around in her bag, whilst Atlas patiently waited for whatever she was doing. Never, ever again, would he ever annoy Lee. She was everything. She was the only thing he could ever need. Who would have thought how much he missed her, being 'trapped' in the bathroom. Lee finally emerged from her backpack, with two ziplocked bags that stank out the entire room the second she pulled them out.

"Wanna get high?"

Atlas gleamed, his head perking up at once. How could he even think about rejecting her? Soon, they were sitting at the bedroom window with a spliff between them. Atlas felt himself ease into it, slowly melting into the floorboards. The fog washed over his brain, wave after wave, burying him deeper into his brain. It only took twenty or so minutes, and then he was completely stoned out of his mind. This was what he needed. Calmness, distance away from his body. He forgot about the cuts. He forgot about the bandages, the bathroom, the blood.

Lee rolled up another spliff for him - how could he say no? Atlas had fucked up, way too much this time, and Eulalie was kind enough to not kick him out, gifting him the weed he wanted so badly instead. She was such a great friend.

He knew he was risking greening out soon - but nothing felt real at all. If this wasn't real, there were no consequences, right? If this wasn't real, nothing could hurt him, nothing could hurt the ill-looking boy he was watching from a third-person perspective.

He glanced over at the woman. She barely had any weed at all; just watching Atlas silently with a small smile placed on her lips. In fact, she only had one hit, and left the rest to the boy. She gave up so much for him, Atlas realised, with guilt burning at his chest again.

Her blue hair flourished in the breezes of the night sky; she was just perfect. Why would Atlas ever think she was a bad friend? The moon shone onto her - highlighting her golden eyes. He never really thought about her eyes - were they real or contacts? He had never met someone with golden eyes. Shuffling closer to Lee, he got lost in her eyes. They lit up with so much love, he could see himself in the reflection. Her eyes weren't golden really, but rather, a beautiful hazel that gleamed when in the sun. She was gold. She was golden.

The boy closed his eyes gently. It was as if he were being pulled back into another part of his brain. He watched the world around him pass by slower than ever, watching through a screen rather than his own eyes. Atlas longed for this dream-like state. He didn't need to think, to feel.

Atlas pulled himself back further as Eulalie guided him to her bed, placing him down cautiously and sitting on his lap. Although his heart beat faster, his mind muffled it. *Just go with it. Just let it happen. It doesn't matter. It wasn't real.*

He felt her hands travel down to his trousers.

Just let it happen. You don't matter. Lee matters.

18 -

Atlas woke up in Lee's bed this time - her body warmth cradling him as he twitched around. This time, he let himself sink into her arms. Whatever this was, it was better than the bathroom. The week of cold isolation... well, it gave him a new appreciation for Eulalie. She was so much better than the bloody tiles and rough bathtub.

The morning sunrise beamed through her curtains, reminding Atlas of his sudden blistering headache and aching eyes; definitely caused by last night.

Last night.. what happened last night? Were they supposed to talk about it? Did he even want to? Did he even remember it right..? The last thing the boy felt present for was when she held his face, sat on his lap, and moved her way down to his trousers. The rest.. no, no he had no idea. Maybe he was better off not knowing.

The unknowingness of Eulalie's actions paralysed him abruptly - how far did she go? Vomit crept up his throat as flashes of images crossed his mind; were they memories from yesterday or just his imagination?

Fuck. What did she do? How was he supposed to know.. what was real, what was just a dream?

The boy's mind brought forward pieces of startling images. Eulalie holding down his legs. He felt his legs - mutilated, bandaged, and now.. bruised. Eulalie kissing him, gentle at first, then rougher. He touched his lips; dry, chapped, and now...now they were red-raw and crusted. Eulalie kissing his neck, so hard it hurt.

Fuck. It was all real.

Atlas jumped up, away from Lee, who only grunted in response, and to the bathroom, which had a mirror. He pointed it to his neck, and.. oh. There it was. A massive hickey sliding down his neck, red and purple and black.

Cut it off. Peel off your skin. Nobody can ever see it - Lee can't see it. Cut it. Scratch it off yourself.

Atlas prodded into his neck. She had been there, her lips had been on him. He felt the sickness coming up even faster now. Disgust crowded up his brain; how could he let her do that? He was such a fucking yes-man.. why didn't he say no or just do anything to fucking stop her?! This was all his fault. He fucking deserved it.

He had to tell her to stop.. or at least, to tone it down. By a lot. Maybe he'd have to get a real job, so he could actually pay her.. so she wouldn't kick him out. He could do other favours, like more chores. Yes - that would be perfect! He wouldn't have to do those stupid things, he hated 'having fun' with her so much.

Atlas lightened up, just a bit, but then, when he realised the room he was in, his eyes widened. The messy, bloodied-up bathroom.

What if, if he mentioned his dislike for her doing.. that.. then, maybe she'd just have enough of him altogether.. and put him in there forever? What if she never talked to him again - didn't even look at him? What if she just left him to starve and die alone in the fucking bathtub? No.. no, god no, it wasn't worth the risk. It wasn't worth being left alone. Lee was so perfect. He just had to deal with it. People weren't perfect, and this was her one flaw.

The boy returned to her bed.

Eulalie was so worth the pain, the discomfort. She was golden, beautiful, caring. Just a small favour for her would never hurt, though his pain would never ever be enough to repay all the amazing things she had done for him. The gifts, the shelter, food, water, love. His pain, no, HE would never be enough. If only he just told Lee this, told her how worthless he really was, then she would kick him out at once. But no, he was the one manipulating her, he was the one emotionally blackmailing her; though he didn't say it in words, it felt like.. *be by my side, or I'll cut myself, shred my skin to pieces. Sit near me, or I won't eat. Watch me closely and carefully, or I'll hurt myself, I'll find a way, I'll fucking do it. I'd tear out my eyes if it meant never seeing you leave.*

How was Eulalie so stupid - so naïve? He was a terrible, awful, disgusting human being. He should have died in the bathroom, choking on his own blood, he would have died on the pavement, freezing and gripping his own skin for a second of comfort or warmth, he should have died on the bridge, his body crushed and distorted, lying pathetically on the road. But most of all, he should have died under the train station stairs. Where his life started, where Lenore's ended. What would Lee think if she knew about Lenore? Atlas basically murdered her. He had blood on his hands, and sacrificing his own was not proving worthy.

But he didn't dare say a word. *Evil, liar, manipulator.* He didn't dare tell her the truth. Because he knew what his life was like without Eulalie. He knew, trapped in the bathroom. *That's* what life was like without her. *That's* what he deserved. Even the thought of losing of Eulalie made him irk forward, his stomach pushing up sick.

Life without Eulalie was cold, lonely, and depressive. Shut, trapped in a tiny room, where only his thoughts were left with him, left with 'what ifs?' and 'where did I go wrong?'. Left in a liminal space, questioning what it would all be like if he didn't just fuck it up. What did he do wrong? Where did he go wrong? What could he have done, if he were thrown back in time a year or so ago? Would he fix himself and forget all about her, or go chasing after all, enjoying all the moments they had together until the imminent failure?

Lee wasn't Lee anymore. She used to be so perfect. She would never yell, never make the boy question himself, but now she was totally different. Who changed her? Was it him? Was he such a horrible human that it just rubbed off onto her? *Disease, disease, disease.*

But she was still his protector. His friend. And life without her wasn't worth living. Without Eulalie, who even was he?

"Atlas, stop looking so fucking miserable," Lee snarled. "What do you have to be sad about? I give you everything and anything." The boy wiped his face clean of any emotion lingering at once. "We're going to do something today. Get dressed."

Atlas got into some clothes he found chucked in the corner of the room, and put them on quickly, aware that Eulalie was watching him. Lee had her hair up this time - he had never seen her go out like this, always with it down, wrapping around her shoulders, but today it was in a messy bun. She wore a baggy hoodie that had food stains all the way down, and plaid trousers that were obviously pyjamas.

"You can't wear that," Eulalie rolled her eyes, looking up and down judgementally at Atlas' equally messy hoodie, and black joggers. "Get changed, you look a right state."

Back-chat or accept it? Back-chat or accept it? She's wearing the same thing as me. She looks more of a 'state'. Back-chat or accept it?

Atlas murmured an apology. Lee handed him some jean shorts and a t-shirt of a band he had never heard of, 'Car Seat Headrest', which the boy immediately slipped into without a word.

"Good!" she exclaimed, starting to unlock the front door now.

"Um, Eulalie?" a small voice echoed, walking towards the woman.

"What's the problem now? Are you-" She stopped, staring at him.

Atlas stood, shaking, hugging himself, attempting to hide. The shirt, slightly small for him and with the short sleeves cut shorter, perfectly revealed every single bandage that was still stuck onto his broken skin - and then the rest of his fresh, scabby and red-raw scars perfectly on show. Eulalie smiled down at his legs, which were in even worse of a state than his arms. Even more scars were visible, even less bandages, and these scars weren't just scars.. they were rips, gashes, hacks, lunges at his own skin. His scars were already starting to raise and split.

"Please.. let me wear something else."

If anyone saw him like this...

"No. You did this, you wanted me to see this, so let's let the world see." Lee opened the door.

"*Eulalie-*"

"You better come follow me right now, or you'll wish you were fucking grateful for what you were just given. I have so many more clothes, or maybe no shorts at all would show off your little accomplishments more."

Atlas gazed up at her, fear struck in his eyes.

"That's what I thought. Come with me."

Though it was only about nine in the morning, there were still a distressing amount of people walking the streets of East Worthing. It was like Lee had purposely gone down all the busiest streets, Atlas didn't doubt for a second she was doing this with full intent. Every single one of them was a potential threat, every single one of them took at least five seconds to stare at Atlas' body, carved, red, disgusting. A little girl with her hair tied up in neat plaits passed, tugging at her mother, who quickly moved her on.

More and more shame built up in every space of the boy's brain. Panic urged and spiked around his body. People were looking, people were staring. *Disgusting, broken, slut.* The boy wanted to crash down to the pavement, and hold himself in a tight ball, so nobody could see him. He clutched at his arms, trying to hide his worst injuries, but Lee, who was looking as if she was having the time of her life, snatched down his arm, making sure to dig her nails into a bandage.

Eulalie reached a point along the sea front, then started walking back again. It was getting busier by the minute, all eyes were on him, somebody was going to say something, somebody was going to attack him. Eventually, they reached the co op right next to her apartment, which was clearly all for liquor, as Eulalie dragged Atlas in and took him directly to the drinks.

"Your reward," she said, pointing to the vast amounts of drinks in an aisle. "Pick some things."

"Spirits?"

"No spirits," she said, firmly. "They're up by the counter behind the lady. Choose something here," Eulalie repeated, her patience obviously growing thin. Atlas, noticing this, quickly pointed at a couple different drinks, ones that he knew that she liked.

"Okay, go take them to the house. I'll go pay," Eulalie smiled, handing him the key to the apartment and walking over to the cashier, who greeted her with a passionate smile. Streams of conversation flooded the store at once - these two obviously knew each other well. Probably because Eulalie was right next door, and her alcohol consumption was regular, and maybe concerning.

Atlas grabbed the three drinks they had agreed on, a cheap boxed wine, some prosecco that they had last time, and had tasted strongly of his own vomit, and then a big glass of co-op brand cider. He placed two of them into his short's pockets, where they stuck out uncomfortably, then he held the boxed wine.

The boy walked out, leaving the two women chatting happily to each other. Lee said that this was his prize.. prize for what? For dealing with the public humiliation? For not cutting himself again? For-

"Hey! You there, boy! Come back here right now!" the old lady yelled fiercely, her whole demeanour switching.

Atlas whipped his head back round, confused. Hadn't Lee paid yet- oh.

He started at Eulalie, who was clearly mouthing the word 'RUN'. The boy sped off at once, carrying all the drinks that he thought Eulalie wanted to buy for him. He unlocked the door, hands shaking, and rushed inside the house, locking it quickly again, and hoping the old lady didn't follow him.

Eulalie returned home about ten minutes later, knocking rapidly at the door.

"You made me steal for you," Atlas murmured, fists clenched, his own nails digging into his hands. *Hold it together. Don't show you're scared - you're angry, you're threatening.*

"Excuse me? I did what I had to." Lee locked the door behind her.

"I'm not your stupid little puppet that you get to steal for you," the boy said, gritting his teeth together. "Don't make me fucking do that again. What if security got my face and my parents saw on the news or some shit?!"

"Oh, *piss off!*" Eulalie shouted. And just like that, with her voice raised, so much more dangerous than him, Atlas felt himself shrink into nothing, again. "Shut the fuck up, Atlas! I'm doing this all for you, can't you *fucking see that*?! Or are you all too wound up in your own world that you can't see I'm doing what's best for you?!"

"By making me steal?" the boy asked, quietly, staring down at his feet.

Eulalie slapped a hand to her forehead, and laughed bitterly. "God! You're so close minded! It's not like that, not at all." The woman grabbed the drinks Atlas had set down on the table, and opened the box of wine with her nails. "Here!" she screamed, shoving it into the boy's chest. "Drink it."

Atlas glared back at her, defiant this time.

"I said fucking drink it, you brat!" Eulalie smacked him, fast, hard, in the cheek.

He took a sip.

"More."

Atlas took another sip.

"*More!*"

He drained half the box of wine in only a few seconds, focussing on not throwing back up the cheap, foul-tasting wine, whilst also trying to ignore the throbbing stinging in his cheek. *If you show weakness, if you show you're hurt, you loose.*

"Finish it."

He threw the now empty box to the ground. "What the fuck do you gain from this?!" Atlas yelled.

She undid the cork-screw of the drink, angrily glaring at the boy. Once undone, she handed it to the boy. "Drink it."

"I don't understand," Atlas cried, feeling his voice break, all anger left of him melt and fuse into fear. "I don't understand!" the boy repeated, tears blurring his vision.

"What don't you understand?" she scoffed.

"Everything! Why did you take me in? Why do you cut yourself? Why are you so fucking nice to me? Why are you a bitch? Why do you care so much? Why don't you give a shit? Why did you lock me in that bathroom? Why did you hurt me? Why did you make me steal for you? Why do you even fucking like me? Why did you get me high? Why are you trying to get me drunk? Why me? Why, and what the fuck actually happened last night?"

His eyes swam with tears - looking up at Eulalie, her face was warped and watery. Her eyes.. so golden, so beautiful.. but so dark, so mean.. so cunning. *Hurt her, hurt her, hurt her.*

"And why can't I hate you?!"

The woman paused, staring at Atlas, apparently too shocked on what to say. What could she say? What could she possibly say that could actually answer his questions? Did he even want to know?

"You can't hate me, because I'm the only one who cares about you. Nobody else even remembers you exist. You're nothing - a shell of a human being. You're just bones now, and by the look of you, you're trying to carve them out so you're less than nothing. The only thoughts in your head; the only thing you can possibly care about, is hurting yourself! I don't think you're even human anymore!

"Now," Eulalie said, gentle this time, "why don't you finish up these drinks? You know it's easier not being sober. For both of us."

So he drank. He did what he was told. Like a dog. A well trained fucking dog. Atlas finished both bottles between hiccups and with a lot more encouragement from Eulalie. The world closed in more, his eyes were fuzzy, glassy and unfocused, his teeth were itchy and dry. As he finished the last drink, suddenly, he realised, it was far too much. His world slowed down at once - the clock ticked loudly, tick.. ..tick. tikc... tkc.. .....tic., slower.

Everything.. was. Very. Dizzy. Very.. very. uh.. very, too much. He was.. too. drunk. Too far. Too much. Too many. She called him a light weight. *Light, skinny. He's too skinny. Too much wrong with.. with him.* Not worth anything. *Worth nothing.* Her voice pounded in his head, pounded, deafening. *It hurts, it hurts.* She hurts. He was a manipulator. *Manipulating her. Evil.* Worth less than nothing. Lee helped him up - with, wobbling. skin and bones. *Worth nothing.* She led him to the room. Her room. Her *bed*. Her covers.

"no. no. no-, i cant. lee. i cant. cant see. i dont. i don't know. what's going on? please - what's happening to me?" *look at me. look at me. whats going on. i cant talk., its , not coming. through, is it? it's not working.*

Her voice bounced off the walls, murmurs and jokes.. but, words. There were no words; just, noises. She spoke a different language - but.. no, it was.. english. he heard sparks of words.. like 'calm'. like,, 'shhh'. that wasn't a word...

hear me. listen. listen to me. hear me. stop it. stop it. please.

Atlas tried shouting, tried screaming. *nothing. nothing at all.* his mouth, open, confused, but no sound came through. his brain. disconnected. broken.

i don't want to, don't want to, don't want it.

Eulalie placed him onto the bed, smiling at his blank expression. They both said nothing, and she lifted up his shirt, throwing it to the side. She pulled down his shorts. She grasped Atlas' hand, placing it on her neck. She held it there tight, grinning - if she let go, his hand would droop back down, like he was dead.

sex with a ghost, a ghost, a corpse i'm not here, im not even there. that cant be me.

disgusting, disgusting, disgusting.

i let this happen. its my fault. i let it happen.

Eulalie took off her shirt, and took down her hair. The second the boy processed her unclothed body, he closed his eyes and brought his awareness back even further, brought his soul back. There was nothing, nobody there left, nobody left in the body of that small, pale little fifteen year old child. There was nobody sitting opposite Eulalie, just the sick and twisted, aching pile of bones, too tired, too black out drunk to even try anymore.

not like this/. not like this. not lkike this. not like thjis. nto liek this. nto lkiethits.

not lkike this.

.,...,

im asexual.

19 -

i think its best to just.. give in.

its all she wants. everyone does it. even fifteen year olds.

she's twenty-six. fifteen year olds don't do it with twenty-six year olds.

but she loves me.

does she?

im asexual.

im disgusting.

The boy wasn't sure what '*woke him up*'. After the drinks, he gave in. He accepted the drink, the weed, and the coaxing without a fuss. It made her happier. It made her less likely to hurt him. But.. this evening. She had gone too far.

It started when Atlas felt sick. He pushed and poked at his meal, much to the woman's detest. He couldn't help feeling anxious, terrified, horrified for whatever she was planning, like he did every night. She tutted, and made a couple snide comments about his body. He never realised how much he had pissed her off that evening, not until..

Eulalie pushed him down. Like usual. She pushed on his arms, sat on his legs, and held him still. She ripped off his shirt, and grabbed his trousers down. Even if he tried, he was powerless. But there was no point trying to get her off - he had learnt that before. Struggling would only cause pain.

This time, this time was different. She walked towards the oven, and took out a scorching, red-hot knife, one she cooked with, handling it gently with an oven glove. She spoke sternly, whispering a threat.

"I want you to do something for me. If you don't, then I'll burn this into your fucking thighs."

At first, he refused. She was disgusting, revolting, evil, awful. He wasn't doing *that* for her. *I'm fifteen. I'm asexual. I'm scared.* Nothing for her. Eulalie was true to her word. She watched, sneering, as Atlas shrieked through his teeth every time the flaming handle was jabbed into his leg. Eulalie watched him flinch desperately away from her, only to be grasped by her long nails, and held in place, as she scorched the burning object onto his thighs repetitively.

Despite his refusal, with the blade melting into his skin, she got what she wanted from him anyway. Despite the threat, the *deal* she proposed, she carried on, doing what she wanted to the boy, whilst sliding the knife theough his thighs. It was all too much - words were impossible, all he knew was *pain*.

 Atlas had thought he had made good friends with pain. It tormented him playfully, showing him he could still feel, that he was still alive. But this wasn't pain. This was *torture*. Excruciating torture that he could never win against. If he reacted, the woman would only grin at him, and press down harder. If he gave her nothing, closed his eyes and tried to space out, dissociate from this mess, she would hit him with the handle, and thrusting it into his limbs. He twitched and rolled on the sofa, like he was having a fit. *It will never stop, it's not stopping, I want to die, let this be the end.*

He shuddered and shook cowardly, creeping further and further out of consciousness. This was too much.. too *much.. too much.*

Eventually, Eulalie got bored of him, and threw the handle at his stomach. It instantly churned against his skin - peeling back his dermis, bubbling into his skin fat, blistering the remaining skin. Torture. This was torture. *How did I get here? This is the end.*

"*Please.*" Atlas wept. His eyes rolled back - promptly vomiting on his own chest. "Please. Take it off me." The handle, searing with disgusting heat, felt as though it was melting into him. His blood spluttered around where the metal sank in.

Eulalie had taken one look at the boy, covered in red and black marks, scabby and dirty, with sick slopping around his chest. She took one look at him, and walked into her bedroom with a smile.

The boy pushed off the metal, scorching his hands in the process, and vomited again, onto the sofa. *How did I end up here? This is too much. I can't handle this. She isn't worth it.*

Maybe it was finally time to leave. To turn his back on her. She didn't really care for him, did she? She just cared for his attention. For his body. For his reaction. He could fix it all.. right now. He could kill himself.

Atlas stared towards the kitchen cabinets. She had hid the knives long ago, but she had *armed* him. He needn't look, not this time. She didn't care anymore, she didn't give a shit about what he did, if he died or not. Nothing mattered. Nothing mattered anymore, just the pain. The release. It's what he needs. A shining of silver met his eyes. The handle sizzled into his hand, flames licking around his fingers. *Control. I have control..* Atlas raised it to his throat.

What would she do with your body?

What? What do you *mean?*

What would she do with it? Come on.. you know what she's like. You know what she's done. What would she do with your body? Think.

A heavy lump of dread filled Atlas' chest. No.. if he ended it here.. he would have even less control. He wouldn't even be able to *try* to say no, being lifeless and bloody on the cold dining room floor. If he let himself die here, well.. what would she do? There was no telling. She was a monster. She'd do anything. Rip his body to pieces, cut it up and send it to his family, feast on his eyes, use his bones as a decoration, his skin as a coat. She would stop at nothing. Even if he was lifeless and bloody on the cold dining room floor. Even if he was dead, she would stop at nothing to destroy him.

He had to leave. Go somewhere else. End it all somewhere she would never find him, not in a lifetime. Let his body rot, remain untouched by humans, unseen by mortals, except only bugs; woodlouse and ants and flies devouring through his flesh.

The door was right there. His escape, right there. The keys were only a meter away, hanging on a shelf. Why hadn't he left, ages ago? Why did he fucking wait? He let this happen. He let Eulalie happen. Why did he wait so long? Wasn't he always, always this angry? Wasn't he always this hurt by her? He never 'got used to it'. He never once felt comfortable with her. So why did he wait? He could have avoided it all.. *I could have been safe.*

Leave her. Walk on. Kill yourself. End it all. Make the world a better place.

The keys were right there. It took no effort to gently take them from the hook. No alarms blared, no dramatic red flashing lights, warning Eulalie he was escaping. Icy cold silence. Did she want him to leave?

Stop thinking about her. It's not about her. Kill yourself, please, do it, now.

With a single click, the door unlocked and drifted open, the wind pushing itself into the apartment. No alarms. No red flashing lights. No Eulalie, screaming, begging, wailing for him to stay. Icy cold silence. She wanted him to leave.

Kill yourself, you need to. Your last gift to everyone.

He left the door open, in a moment of defiance. After all these months, pleading to be invisible, and to not exist, the boy was pathetic enough to want her attention. Leave the door open wide enough to show you've left, to show it wasn't a mistake. 'Try' to kill yourself, but 'fail', and let them deal with the mess.

Attention seeker, attention seeker, do it now.

How could he have not seen the fucking signs?! He should had left the second Eulalie placed a single hand on him, a fucking fifteen year old. When Eulalie was fifteen, Atlas was only four years old. How could he not have seen the dangers? Was he really that stupid - that desperate for a motherly figure, that desperate for someone like Lenore to come back into his life?!

Lenore, Lenore, I'll join you soon. Please, hold on, wait for me. I love you more than anything.

Atlas climbed down the stairs to the apartment, clutching every bone in his body that throbbed and shook in pain. She hurt him. She *hurt* him, and he forgave her?! She hit him, cut him, slapped him, scratched him, burnt him, and he *forgave her*?! Rage bubbled with anxiety, pushing the boy even further. He had no energy, none at all, just pure adrenaline, keeping him walking, keeping him alive. For now.

He walked, on and on. The moon shone threateningly over a the deep, black seas - crashing into each other, angry, hurt, damaged. Skies told him that it was dead midnight, dead night-time, dead dusk. The gleams of the moon made him feel something. Something Atlas hadn't felt for a while but he didn't know what it was, but what he did know is that he wanted more.

He stopped at a quiet part of the beach, where the waves were slower, calmer, yet still hurt. This was the place. This was where he was going to kill himself.

Eulalie would kill him if they knew he was out this late. Eulalie would kill him if they found out he had gone back to his old habits. Eulalie would kill him. Metaphorical. Metaphorical, right?

How long would it have been, how long would it have taken, how many more nights, until Eulalie murdered him?

The boy grasped his knife, held cautiously under his jacket. His jacket. Bought by Eulalie. She worked hard to buy this. Maybe she wasn't even that bad. Was he overreacting?

Shut up. You know what she did. I can help you, we can escape it.

His hands shook as he raised the blade higher, ready to be struck into his chest. The pain would be unimaginable. Like a fire squirming inside his guts, spreading across his entire body, burning it to ashes, until he felt nothing. The pain scared him, for the first time ever, but not because of the intensity. Because it would be the last thing he'd ever feel.

Do it. Strike. This is the only way.

How did I end up here?

This is the end. Everything bad, it's all done. This is it. This is the end. And this is what he wanted. After all these months, these failed attempts. It's finally, for Gods' sake, its finally fucking over. He was out.

Three.

This is the end. We all knew it would come to this. Why are we even surprised?

Two.

He could almost hear Lenore calling his name, greeting him with a hug.

One.

Lenore.

A single sunflower floated onto his lap. It shined up at him, the bright yellow unaffected by the murky night sky.

His shining sunflower. His cool breeze. His angel. Staring right back up at him.

Lenore.

She wouldn't want this for me.

What am I fucking doing?

Do it.

I can't. She's right there. I can't do it in front of her.

It's a sunflower.

"It's her." Atlas choked out, breaking out of his own thoughts. "It's you, isn't it?" he said, crouching over.

"Lenore," he repeated, words strangling themselves; tied up in a knot of terror.

He prodded the flower, like he expected it to do something.

"*LENORE.*" Atlas screamed.

The boy didn't realise the sharp clang of a blade, hitting the concrete, and falling down into a rocky mess. The only thing that mattered, all of a sudden, was Lenore. She was here with him. She was right there.

The boy clung on tight to the sunflower's stem, like a child would to their mother's leg.

Don't let go, don't leave me, don't let go.

"Lenore, please.. say something,"

He shook the flower, exhausted, scared. Why wasn't she doing anything? Why was she here?

"Lenore. Please. I'm sorry. I'm not going back."

Blisters burnt into his body, bruises suffocated his limbs.

"Lenore. Everything hurts."

A hundred or so metres back, an old man saw a sickly skinny, bruised, cut up boy, screaming into a sunflower. His *shining sunflower.*

Printed in Great Britain
by Amazon

47683753R00175